CRIG

THE WRAITHS OF TIME

Nanette Ackerman & Charles Ackerman Berry

First published in 2023 by Blossom Spring Publishing
CRIGGA: The Wraiths of Time Copyright © 2023
Nanette Ackerman and Charles Ackerman Berry
ISBN 978-1-7384130-5-8
E: admin@blossomspringpublishing.com
W: www.blossomspringpublishing.com

I shall always be grateful to Charles Ackerman Berry for this wonderful story, and to my husband for his constant support.

VENTURING

In the early autumn of 1883, a stranger came to Crigga, innocently unaware of the part he was destined to play in the continuing saga. Even after so many years, Simon Jeffries' occupation of Greywalls, the house he had built on the headland, remained uneasy. He was wary of allowing visitors to share his haven, but there were occasional exceptions.

One such visitor was Philip Wickenham. Wickenham, a young man of pleasant face and artistic appearance, was a poet. Jeffries was his publisher, and Philip, a year back, had married Catherine – Jeffries' favourite niece. It was a sensitive situation – art and domesticity proving doubtful companions. When the poet first visited the village of Crigga, he knew nothing of the drama which preceded him, or that it was destined to colour the prime of his adult life.

There was a crisis in Wickenham's affairs and, as he waited at Paddington station that September morning, he contemplated the trip with mixed feelings. Things had not been going well at either extreme. Though he welcomed the break, he suspected Jeffries' motive. His uncle-in-law was too shrewd not to have noticed the drift, too forthright to do nothing. Plus, to his mind, a few days together in his Cornish retreat would be an ideal setting for airing the problems. The confrontation had been easily arranged, since Catherine was not fond of travelling.

Yet Philip put worries aside on the train, symbolically moving toward newer, and perhaps better scenes, as it began puffing and groaning out of the station. It was his first visit to Cornwall, and it was impossible not to feel the expectant thrill as the wheels spun faster towards the

Duchy, with its magnificent vistas, 'ghoulies and ghosties', and in particular, Jeffries' rocky bastion at Crigga.

The spell was gently but irrevocably cast on the journey. The carriage was stuffy and when, after some hours of travelling, the train halted at Teignmouth, he noticed the girl. She was a petite, proud little figure, waiting patiently by a carriage door to embark. She carried no ordinary luggage but was clutching a bundle of close-wrapped possessions tightly to her side. Her dress was threadbare but almost painfully clean. Her headscarf betrayed wisps of silky brown hair. Her bearing drew the glances of all on the platform, but it was the set of her features that held Philip transfixed. Her face was pale, ethereal as a ghost and, though her head was held high, she was clearly in deep sorrow, for her eyes were swollen and bore the smudged shadows of weeping. Friendly hands at last assisted her into the shelter of the compartment and the train was signalled away.

The placidity of mind Wickenham had been trying to cultivate suddenly shattered, his thoughts permeated by the memory of the plaintive appeal on her face. Speculation racked him. Who was she? Where was she from and where was she going? What unhappy circumstances had induced her to travel alone in such obvious grief? He could find no answers and, at last, he forced himself to concede that, whatever the solutions were, they were no business of his.

By the time he had exhausted his reverie, a greatly shortened train was well on its way. The rails were now an intrusion, twin serpents striking at the very vitals of solitude, the starkly new branch-line to Crigga an elongated scar along the plump limb of the Cornish peninsula. Yet the wound seemed to emphasise the unsullied loveliness that spread into green distance on either side of the track.

Soon the engine was cutting and snorting through deep cuttings and up tortuous inclines, and then, easing across a lofty viaduct spanning a colourful valley, the train entered a prospect of seaward eminences and wind-humbled gorse. The cliffs of Crigga came into sight like gigantic buffers at journey's end, and with a last triumphant gasping of steam, the long haul was over.

There had been a change of train and many stops on the final leg of the journey, leaving only a very few passengers to disembark at the terminus. By the time Philip had got his cases and stepped down from the carriage, the platform was empty – except for the stationmaster in conversation with a traveller at the exit gate. Philip had half expected to see the authoritative presence of Jeffries, but the real disappointment was the absence of the girl from Teignmouth, who he had subconsciously assumed would be travelling to Crigga, but had apparently disembarked unseen at one of the stations on route. Wryly, smothering a wave of chagrin, he began to walk to the barrier.

It may have been due to the sultry weather and the contrast between this remote spot and the bustle of London, but to Philip it seemed an almost uncanny peace that lay over the station, a pervading air of expectancy which had nothing to do with mundane things, but was more like the hush before thunder, or the pause along the crest of a breaking wave. The faint whisper of steam from the resting engine and the distance voices of the two men by the barrier, only served to accentuate the brooding atmosphere. Through the fence railings he caught a glimpse of the yard, where the motif of silent desertion also prevailed. There was no sign of Jeffries, no sight or sound of conveyances, no suggestion of normal activity at all.

'Tes the fish,' the stationmaster was saying, as though in reply to Philip's unspoken questioning. '*You* d' know, Chegwidden, ent nothing a mortal man can do about they, for nigh on twenty years they've come regular, but this time they'm late. Ent no telling with they.'

The passenger, whom later Philip was to recognise as the village innkeeper, waved a hand fretfully at a collection of goods he had ventured to Plymouth to buy.

'So, the cry still ent gone up?'

'No, they still ent come.'

'Tom ent brought the jingle nor nothin'?'

'*Nothin*'.'

The stationmaster was infinitely patient. He squinted askance at Philp, subconsciously fingering a bright row of buttons on his uniform. 'You d' know how it be, Chegwidden. Best leave the parcels till later. You d' know how it be'. Then, turning to Wickenham, 'Tes the same for 'ee all, sir. They'm out there, a-waitin' the cry for the fish.'

'No jingles', apparently meant no transport, though Jeffries had promised to have him met, and was finicky about such niceties. Philip began to explain this, and at once noticed a change in their manner. They looked doubtfully at him, then exchanged sour glances. There was momentary silence, then obligations of high office overruled the stationmaster's repugnance.

'Ah, that'll be Shaddy Bunt,' he said shortly. 'Shaddy may come, and Shaddy mayn't come. Ent no knowing with Shaddy. Else you'd best leave the bags at the station and walk.'

Philip tried not to seem chastened, 'And where do I find Greywalls?'

Chegwidden grunted, with a dismissive gesture towards the station yard, 'Greywalls, ezza? Ent no missing the grey house.' He spoke with the inherent bitterness Wickenham was to recognise wherever Jeffries, Greywalls or any of their concern, were mentioned. 'There she do be, like a great wart on the headland for too many good Crigga folk to see'. He spat dry with eloquence, 'And I'll give 'ee a good day'.

A brief nod to the stationmaster, and he was through the barrier and away. The official, too, turned his back, muttering about pressure of duties elsewhere.

'Shaddy Bunt may come if the call ent up,' were his cryptic words. 'Best wait in the yard for'un if 'ee ent going to walk.'

Philip, mystified, but with a growing sense of occasion, strolled to the forecourt where, clear of the station, he viewed for the first time the magnificent panorama of Crigga and its encircling bay.

Crigga had changed little during the years. It was still virtually unknown – the railway so far having had scant effect on village life. The station yard could not have been more than fifty yards from the cliff edge. Beyond, lay the prospect that had charmed generations: the watery blue dappled with white, enclosed by the wild tumble of rocky promontories culminating at the northern tip in the great guardian of cliff, now screened by the evening's haze. At its southern aspect, the shoreline mellowed gradually downwards to the hollow containing the village and harbour, rising again in presumed grandeur to project the second arm of the bay, where the mighty headland nuzzled into the sea like a huge, humped monster. Midway along the middle slope of the beast, as Chegwidden had promised, petty against its surrounds but prominently visible, was the grey house, starkly intrusive against the weathered background of turf and rock.

All this Wickenham absorbed in a second, then his eyes were drawn to the foreground where, towards the harbour side of the view, he glimpsed the tense group of watchers – clustering along the prominences of the cliffs. Their gaze was fixed endlessly on the watery distance. Mostly they stared in silence, pregnant with the expectation that Philip had sensed in the station but, even as he gazed in bewilderment at the whole tableau, the spell was broken by the appearance of a little pony and trap that jingled and clopped up the slope from the village. Twice the conveyance halted for the driver to have words with the watchers. They seemed ill-pleased at the interruption, and a drift of rising annoyance floated across.

'Darn 'ee, Bunt, get 'ee along. You do know darn well the cry ent gone up.'

Unperturbed, Shaddy absorbed the rebuff, returned a crude pleasantry, and encouraged the pony to a brisk trot towards the station. He dismounted as he pulled up by Philip.

Long ago, in the sole cause of bounty, Shadrach had defected to Jeffries. He had grown into a short stubby little man who now presented himself in a worn jersey, and clearly bequeathed trousers too big for him. His small, darting little eyes acknowledged no respect for standing or class. One seaward eye on the cliffs, he was anxious to get his assignment over as soon as possible. He greeted Philip with a look of rejecting nonchalance.

'Be 'ee the mister from Lunnon, then?' And when Philip nodded, 'Ent got no time for that there Lunnon. Ent 'ee brought any bags, then?'

'There – in the station.'

'How did 'ee leave 'un in there, then?' He relented and shuffled towards the platform. 'Get 'ee into the jingle, then mister,' he ordered over his shoulder, 'else the cry'll be up, you.'

Philip stepped into the tiny vehicle, his thoughts a piquant mixture of amusement, wonder and regret. The

6

regret stemmed from the recurring frustration that the girl he had glimpsed at Teignmouth should so quickly pass out of his life, her story unknown to him. How maddening that one fleeting facet of one person, in one moment, could shine from the multitude, then disappear forever like a wisp in the sun. But the Fates make no such fundamental errors. He turned, in one last look around, and there she stood, still clutching her bundle, like a materialisation from a dream. He was yet to find that the unconsidered raising of visions can only lead to more and more impossible imaginings.

His elusive fellow passenger had wandered from the opposite side of the station, where, like himself, she had been hoping to find a messenger or transport. Unlike Philip's the search had been unsuccessful, and now she looked utterly spent. There was an unspoken appeal on her face as she gazed at him.

Shaddy had just arrived with the bags and was about to load them into the jingle when Philip stopped him, 'Hold on. Do you know that young lady? Is she a Crigga girl?'

Shadrach had already spotted the newcomer. He tilted his cap to scratch his head and pondered, 'No, she ent a Crigga maid.' He was half puzzled, half evasive.

'She needs help,' Philip said.

Shaddy fiddled with his cap again, uneasily, 'Best not to have any truck with she, mister.'

'Why ever not?'

'Best not, that's all.'

'Nonsense,' Philip said, brusquely. 'The poor girl is out on her feet. We must do something.'

But still Bunt objected. 'Mister Jeffries won't like 'un. Ent no room with this luggage, anyways.'

'Oh, be quiet, man,' Philip snapped. 'She must be helped to the village at least. I shall handle objections.

The bags can be fetched later. Put these back in the station while I see to the lady.'

Shaddy complied, muttering darkly against 'furriners who 'don't know where they'm to.'

Wickenham hurried across to the girl, just in time to support her from actual collapse. With a reassuring word he dismissed her faint protests and assisted her into the jingle. Shaddy returned and they set off at last for the village, along the narrow road skirting the cliff.

With the onset of dusk, the watchers on the heights were beginning to drift away, weary with the strain of waiting. Many were curious, with resentful glances at the occupants of the little conveyance as it clattered past, but nobody spoke – except occasionally against Shaddy's constant query about the fish.

'Get 'ee along, Shadrach,' one growled bluntly. Ent having no truck with the likes of '*ee*.' Clearly, the little Cornishman's role working for Jeffries put him beyond the pale of good Crigga folk.

Again, Philip wondered about the strange preoccupation with the fish. If there were boats in the harbour and fish in the sea, why weren't men out at sea catching them? 'But the fish ent come,' was the cry, 'The cry ent gone up,' the repeated lament – though surely the bay must be full of them.

What cry had not gone up, and why had it not? And what good was it doing to lurk idly on the cliffs? He might have asked Shaddy, but Shaddy had already dismissed him as an ignorant Londoner, and Philip had more on his mind. The young lady had now recovered to stammer her thanks, and the riddle of her arrival took precedence over the conundrum of the fish. Shadrach who, in between arguing with the fisherman, had been gawping at her, and had no compunction about questioning.

'What's to do, maid? Where have 'ee come from, then?'

'Devon.' Her voice was surprisingly cultured and soft, and she spoke as though from within a dream.

'Ent got no time for that Devon,' said Bunt, for whom any place beyond the Crigga milestone remained an alien land, 'And where be a-going, then?'

Very quietly she replied, 'Fore Street,' and then, hesitantly, 'to the Pemberthy cottage.'

'Pemberthys, ezza?'

The answer, after a long pause, came even more softly, with a fresh welling of tears to her eyes, 'I am their grandchild.'

'Darned if I didn't hear so.' Shaddy struck his thigh in revelation, 'You be Sara, the little maid Pemberthy, ess?'

'Not Pemberthy. Michal.' She spoke now with a tired flourish of pride that made Shaddy shuffle and blink, 'I'm Sara Michal,' she said.

Shaddy shook his head. 'How do 'ee make that out?' he began. But Philip, equally puzzled, intervened.

'That's enough,' he warned, 'Leave the young lady alone.'

Suddenly, he had the strange imaging that fingers of sea mist crept up from the further cliff-top and were beckoning. Then they held motionless in the fading light.

The journey continued in silence, leaving Wickenham more puzzled than ever. He would always remember that evening; the sun's aftermath disappearing seawards, twilight beginning to shroud the great arc of the bay, the lazy clatter of hooves in tune with the tinkling bells, the fading breeze ruffling Sara's tumble of brown hair. But for all the tranquillity, there was still an atmosphere of foreboding, the menace of slumbering dragons in the brooding sky and the now sullen swell of the sea. It was the same sense that had pervaded the station, something that almost came through the physical senses yet hovered to catch breath on the threshold of known things.

They were close to the village now, descending a winding track with the harbour coming into view on their right. The ancient backbone of dwellings arched along the cliff road into Fore Street, with the square and the central inn as the pivot. The spine ran parallel to – and in parts nearly overhung – the cliff edges on the seaward side, while to landward irregular straggles of cottages sprawled from the main thoroughfare.

At one of the older cottages, squat built of stone and tile, its whitewash scarred by the ravages of sun and storm, Shaddy reined in the pony. He was uneasy, his eyes darting warily at the villagers who trudged by, viewing the jingle with open curiosity and mistrust.

'Here, maid,' he muttered, 'here be Luke Pemberthy's place.'

A knot of people was already gathering near the dwelling, the news of Sara's arrival having rapidly filtered along the line of watchers and, from this group, two men detached themselves and approached. One was tall and elderly, the other of medium build and young middle-age. Both looked suspiciously at Wickenham and the girl.

'And 'ere do be Luke Pemberthy and Joe Pendenna,' Shaddy told her. Then with a defensive tone in his voice, 'It do be alright Luke. Here be the maid. She be spent, Luke. Mister did but give her a lift from the station.'

Both men silenced him with a glare. 'Hold your tongue,' the elder admonished, 'Do 'ee think I've no mind to look after my own?'

Sara showed no inclination to speak. She sat pale and tense, anxiously clasping her hands as the fishermen drew closer, and at last looked up into the questioning face of her grandfather. Luke Pemberthy's features had grown to be like the crags he lived among – rugged in outline, worn from the impact of spray and wind, mellowed by the same elements that battered them. His tall frame was bowed now, weathered with worry, wearied from toiling for the fish that came and searching for the fish that did not come – yet his eyes still shone clear and their depths held a measure of gentleness.

'Don't 'ee mind, Shaddy Bunt,' he said reassuringly, 'he be daft as a brush. We couldn't come away from they fish, don't 'ee see?' He offered a roughened hand to Sara, 'Come little maid. Poor Missus be vexed so she don't know where'm to. But cums along in, and we'll look after 'ee proper.'

It was then that Philip glanced toward the cottage and saw the old woman and, of all the varied happenings of that strange day, this sight affected him most. She stood on the step, framed in the doorway, a bent crone shrouded in a shawl with wisps of grey hair straggling against a background of flickering firelight. But it was her face that fascinated and shocked him beyond reason, for she directed a stare of such bitter hate – first at him and then at the girl – that made her eyes glow in the half-light.

Never had he experienced such utter malignance and for a moment a chill ran through him. It was as though she embodied – in one vitriolic second – the entire essence of Crigga's resentment. Understandable perhaps regarding himself, but why should she have visited it upon her own grandchild?

'Mother!' Luke's voice rose gruffly, 'How don't 'ee come and welcome the little maid?' But Elizabeth, disassociating herself from the scene with a dismissive gesture and with a last acid glance at Wickenham, turned and re-entered the cottage.

'Cums 'ee in, maid,' Pemberthy said huskily. 'Granny be that mazed just now.' He put out an arm to assist her, 'Joe, do 'ee bring the maid's things.'

Philip, who with instinctive helpfulness had automatically reached for the bundle, at once found the fisherman's grip on him, forcing his hand away. Flushed with a mounting frustration, he met the warning gaze of the Crigga man, 'Ent no call for 'ee here,' said Pendenna briefly. 'Best be gone, mister, or trouble there'll be.'

Philip could only watch helplessly as the trio made their way into the cottage, Sara timorously on the arm of her grandfather, Joe with the bundle slung over his shoulder in total rejection of the jingle, its occupants, and all that it stood for. Sara turned once to murmur faint thanks as they went into the cottage, leaving Philip chastened and sore at himself, while Shaddy encouraged the pony along the last half mile or so to the grey house.

The vista as they mounted the rise was magnificent, with the Pennan headland visible to the south and Greywalls looming ahead, and at any other time Philip would have been enraptured. But for him the magic had gone from the evening, his thoughts engrossed in images of his own making. Since Sara's pathetic departure, his mind was seething with a new rush of questions. There was obviously an intriguing slant to the Pemberthy story, and though Shaddy, too, was subdued, Philip ventured to ask him. 'What is the matter back there? Is the young lady in some kind of trouble?'

Shaddy turned sullenly away. 'Ent no business of strangers.' He spoke no more till the pony had trotted the remaining yards to the grey house and wheeled through the gates to the great main door. Then he gestured towards the entrance, 'This be it, then. Clements'll 'look out for 'ee now.'

It was Jeffries who appeared on the threshold, a large be-whiskered figure, bluffly apologetic. 'Come in, come along in, Philip my boy.' He thrust out a hand in greeting. 'Would have met you myself, but you see how it is, eh, eh? And with the luggage, barely enough room. What?' he wondered as Philip descended, 'Where the deuce are the bags, eh?'

'My fault.' Philip felt strangely guilty. 'Shaddy will have to go back for them. I gave someone a lift from the station.'

'A *lift*?' Jeffries echoed, 'The devil you did. Crigga folk accepting a lift? No station wagon around, I suppose. The damn fish.'

'You, too?' Philip asked. 'What *is* all this bother about fish?'

'Damn their eyes,' Jeffries snorted. 'Before you leave Crigga, you'll know all there is to know about fish. But let's get indoors.'

'I hope,' Philip pressed, 'you do not object about the lift. Shaddy seemed afraid you would.'

'Nonsense. Man's a fool. Delighted to help if I can, eh? But the rascals won't usually take my help.'

'So I gathered.' Philip followed Jeffries into the hall where a prim middle-aged woman was waiting, starchy in a white apron, regarding his advent with bland unconcern.

'Clements,' announced Jeffries, 'Excellent creature. Rules like a queen over this cosy kingdom – eh, Clements?'

The hall, like the rest of the house was pure Jeffries – wealthy bachelor Jeffries. It was deep carpeted, panelled in oak, tastefully hung with paintings and tapestries, and strewn with the more personal objects – stout walking sticks, a shrimping net and one or two rods. On a table reposed a variety of plants and an assortment of books.

A slight sense of inferiority in the shade of the publisher's strong personality was normal for Philip, but tonight he happily allowed himself to be directed and cossetted as his host willed.

'A wash and a brush and we'll dine,' said Jeffries, 'Nothing formal, my boy. Good Cornish fare and a pitcher of wine, eh? Clements will show you your room.' At his nod, the housekeeper silently led the way upstairs.

The apartment was luxurious, beautifully furnished, set at the corner of the house with two windows – one overlooking the bay, the other the village. Philip removed the dust and grime of the journey and returned downstairs.

They dined in a room bright with candelabra and oil lamps of polished brass. In every way Jeffries had contrived a cheerful compromise between elegant sophistication and homeliness and the meal reflected the pattern, with the palate further sharpened by fine wine from London. Afterwards, lounging in an armchair in the chintzy drawing room and savouring a giant cigar, Jeffries looked contentedly at Philip.

'Well Philip?'

'A wonderful place and an excellent meal. Real Cornish style. The pasty and the fish were delicious.'

'Ah, the fish. It should be.' Jeffries haloed himself

with smoke, 'It was caught only today.'

Philip grimaced, 'I wonder they managed it – all stuck on the cliffs like that.'

Jeffries waited a while before answering, studying the ash of his cigar, 'There's a lot to be learnt about Crigga, my boy. They don't do these things without purpose. The fish …' He paused again. 'That means the pilchards – haven't arrived yet. Damn it.'

Philip was puzzled, 'Why? How can this affect *you*?'

'It can, it can. Damn things shoal close inshore, every summer. Then everything else stops – for the one big catch. They dare not miss the shoals, you see – or their main living is lost. *That's* what they're waiting for. At the sighting the cry goes up for the coming of the fish. Till then everything is tenterhooks.'

'I still don't see. Why should it bother *you*?'

Jeffries shrugged. 'Because, my dear chap, when the fish come late, they blame it – like as not – on me.'

'But that's rubbish.'

'The whole damn world knows it's rubbish – aside from the Crigga folk. Try telling them that. Oh, it's not only the fish. I won't go into the whole thing now but, since I laid the very first brick of this house, most of the things that go wrong in the village are blamed on Greywalls. Half superstition, half natural resentment. We're not popular, not at all.' He sucked pensively on the cigar.

Philip sensed a story, but this was not the time to delve for it. 'And this includes visitors, I suppose?'

'Ah, so you've noticed it.'

'There was a definite atmosphere on the way here.'

'Time may improve things,' Jeffries grunted, 'but so far it hasn't, damn them. That's why I can only employ a fellow like Bunt. Watch out for him, by the way. He's a strange, unpredictable creature – daft if you ask me.'

'And Clements?'

'Clements, I recruited from Truro. Lucky to get either of 'em. No cause for alarm, of course, but keep your chin well in as you go around – at least till those fish come in.'

'You can rely on me,' Philip promised, but Jeffries next words ruffled his calm.

'So,' his host mused, 'who the deuce *was* it accepted a lift, eh?'

Philip felt the colour rise his cheeks. He attempted to speak indifferently. 'Actually, it was a girl.'

Jeffries eyed him with interest, 'A gal? Eh? What girl?'

Philip hastened to justify himself, 'She travelled from Teignmouth. She was adrift when we got here. I couldn't have ignored her.'

'No, no, of course not. But a gal, travelling alone to Crigga?'

'Well, there it is. There's no more to the story.'

'But it doesn't add up, eh? Or does it?' A trace of concern hardened his voice. 'Where did you leave this gal?'

'At a fisherman's – The Pemberthy cottage.'

'Pemberthy? Teignmouth? My God, not that again.' Just for a few seconds Jeffries seemed perturbed. 'What was she like – this girl?'

Philip briefly described Sara. 'But why?' he asked, puzzled. 'I gave her a lift. Surely anyone would. What's wrong?'

'Nothing, of course, on the face of it.'

'Then?'

Jeffries' brows puckered, 'Village scandal,' he grunted, 'Girl's mother ran off with a stranger. Hell of an upset. Now the daughter turns up with a stranger. Innocent, of course, but don't you see?' He gestured down Philip's protests. 'I know, I know, all done in

16

innocence, but with these people – a tricky business. Best to keep clear. Do you see?'

Philip saw. A little at least of the jigsaw began to fall into place. He would have asked further questions, but Jeffries, with a strangely tense air, guided the conversation elsewhere. Later, he nonchalantly began to direct it towards Catherine – through a gleam in his eye that presaged a future fire.

'I thought,' he said, 'you might have brought her along with you.'

Philip knew this was a lie – a bland, diplomatic untruth, but a lie, for Jeffries wanted him there alone.

'You know she's at her sister's,' he said.

'Yes, of course – her sister. Well, it's a pity, the trip would have done you both good.'

'You know she hates leaving London,' Philip countered, 'She would never travel this far.'

Philip was silent, irritated. Jeffries doted on his niece, an added nuisance for the poet. While his host paused to perform the ritual of choosing, cutting, and carefully igniting another cigar, he pondered once more his life's greatest mistake.

Five years had passed since he had met and wooed Catherine, knowing that as Jeffries' favourite niece she was an avenue to literary advancement. This, however, had been incidental. She was attractive and had an air of spoilt nervousness that at first attracted him. But few were surprised when soon after the wedding his first volume of verse appeared bearing Jeffries' imprint.

Since then, he had known something of both worlds, a minor literary success, and the bonds of a union he increasingly yearned to break. Like many before him, by scrabbling for the stars he had fallen into a pit of his own making. Catherine with conventionalism, striking no answering fire from the spark of his creative ambitions.

Largely an honourable man, he had done his best to keep the bargain, but as in all compromise, each ingredient tended to weaken the other. Despite all his efforts to adapt and conform, Catherine was not truly happy, and both knew in their hearts that his work was suffering, for no poet could soar to the heights while trailing one leg on the ground.

'But never mind that now. We'll discuss Catherine later,' Jeffries was saying – as though reading his guest's thoughts. He turned the conversation to books and at length – to Philip's relief – rose and stretched himself, 'Yes, still a lot to be said,' he yawned, 'about Catherine, the way things are going, your next volume of verse, eh? But you're tired after the journey, and it's time for bed. Tomorrow we'll chance our luck and I'll show you something of Crigga, eh? Goodnight then, my boy. Goodnight.'

But Philip rested little that night. The dourly hospitable Clements had put a warming pan in his bed, the sheets were inviting, there was every inducement to slumber, yet though weary through travelling, his mind was obstinately alert.

For a while he lay listening to the muffled roar of the sea and the wind soughing around the eaves. The house seemed too new for traditions of hauntings, yet he sensed a suffusing atmosphere from the past – as though time had curled back on itself to link him with distant days. It was the feeling he had known on the station, all through the jingle ride and the Greywalls evening – something withheld but imminent.

He rose and peered out on the darkened bulk of the bay, at the comforting blink of a far lighthouse and the nearer glow of the green harbour light. Landward, nothing could be seen of the sleeping village, except one or two lights from candles or old-fashioned rush lamps that still glimmered feebly from un-shuttered windows. He went back to bed, his thoughts a maze of wonder and full, not of London, or Catherine, or Crigga itself, but of a girl coming wearily home, of a grandmother turning away from her, and of his hand and the fisherman's hand symbolically trying to grasp the bundle of her treasured possessions.

GREYWALLS

Whatever plans Jeffries may have had for his guest's first day were cancelled by the kind of weather only the British Summer can produce, for Wickenham had woken to a prospect straight out of November – the windows slashed and blurred with driven rain, beyond them a grey sea shipped by half a gale into a maelstrom of tumbling spray. No watchers were to be seen on the cliffs. The very pilchards could be imagined cowering before the storm.

The rain persisted relentlessly, making it impossible to venture far outside, and Jeffries' laments were almost as fierce as the elements. Eventually he conceded defeat and arranged for a fire to be lit in the library, to which they retreated for the rest of the day. It was a large room with a western outlook, its comparative newness over-ridden by the warm tang of leather and the rich mustiness of well-thumbed books. Philip was naturally disappointed at the postponement of the Crigga tour, but in retrospect those hours spent with Jeffries proved one of his happiest memories. After the recent strains it was good to relax, and there was a childlike pleasure in being able to sit comfortably inside with the tempest beating impotently against the warm haven.

Jeffries, too, responded to the snug atmosphere. Towards the end of lunch, topped by a memorable wine, his conversation touched on Greywalls, Crigga, and local lore. It continued in that vein hour after hour, while Philip leaned back and recreated the scenes in the spluttering flames of the fire.

Jeffries was a good raconteur and he had a fund of tales about Crigga – of its ghoulies and ghosties, superstitious beliefs and of the first abortive attempts of building a harbour, of ancient wreckers and smugglers and feuds with the excise men. And, of course, of the pilchards – how for hundreds of years they had annually shoaled in the shallows of Crigga Bay, to be sighted by the headland huers who raised the cry, and from the heights guided the hurrying boats to surround and contain the catch. Some years were good, some bad, sometimes the fish came early, sometimes late, but never in all these centuries had they failed to arrive at last.

'Just my luck,' Jeffries mourned ruefully, 'that when I first came here the damned things started playing up.' He crossed to the window where dusk again menaced the view. 'And they haven't arrived today, that's a certainty. If we hadn't heard the tumult ourselves, Shaddy Bunt would have told us.' He corrected himself wryly, 'Or rather, he wouldn't have been here to tell.'

'And they really blame you?'

'I've told you. They blame me for everything. I'm a ready-made hate symbol. Myself, the house, and all that therein dwell!' He became voluble again, once more recounting his long and bitter fight to establish his dream home on this wild promontory; the labour difficulties, the sly damage to the developing structure at night, the rights of way blocked, the demonstrations to hinder the imported workers. 'Even a touch of the evil eye,' he said, semi-seriously. 'There's an old crone in the village. Came up here once to cry death on the house and its strangers: "If Crigga folk don't get 'ee," she said, Crigga will. And Crigga can wait". Gave me the creeps, Crigga itself, the avenging doom. Sometimes, up here, you can almost believe it.'

Philip, to the scream of the wind and the dark aspect of storm through the rain-battered windows, *could* credit it. 'It's a haunting place,' he confessed. But Jeffries turned back to the saga of Greywalls. There had been scuffles galore, and one major riot on which he seemed reluctant to dwell.

'Damn bad business,' he grunted, 'Best told and forgotten, eh? Had almost finished the place. They broke inside, sent the scaffolding crashing. Injured a few, one poor devil killed outright. Their fault, of course, but damn bad show.'

'When was this?'

'Eh? Years ago – 1863 – I think it would be. Damn near the end of me.' His brow furrowed in grim recollection. 'Rounded up a few of the ringleaders. Fined one or two, but what the hell, they couldn't pay. I let it go. Thought it might improve relations. What a hope, eh?'

'And this was all because of the fish?'

'Eh? Eh?' Jeffries waved down the query. 'Not quite as simple as that. The fish, the house, superstition, and other things. Done with. Best forgotten, eh?'

Philip sensed a story within a story, something too important not to be hinted at, too near conscience to be revealed. No more was said on the matter, yet he retained the impression that a thread had been momentarily exposed and glossed over.

Even after the sacking of the near completed house, Jeffries had not surrendered. Finally, the image his inward eye had glimpsed, materialised fully in timber and stone, and Greywalls straddled the headland – a cuckoo on the Crigga nest.

To the local community, undisturbed for centuries in their rockbound retreat nurtured in superstition, the visitation remained ominous. 'No good will come of 'un,' the elders solemnly warned, a prediction immediately given substance by the worst storm in memory, a series of accidents connected with the house itself, and an indifferent fishing season. In the same winter snow – rare on that stretch of coast – struck with blizzard force, isolating the cottages and farmsteads, bringing hardship to hundreds and even death to some. Linked with a personal tragedy, it would have taken far less than this unhappy chain of events to persuade the fisherfolk that the tall grey house was anything but an emblem of misfortune among them. Children were brought up to regard it so. The shadow of Jeffries monster hung ominously over the village, permeating it with inerasable atmosphere of doom. However mellowed Greywalls grew with the passing years, no matter how accustomed people grew to its brooding presence, between them and it, the great gulf was forever fixed.

It was against this sombre background that fate dangled Wickenham like a puppet to play out the most vital months of his life. But today, at least, the grey house granted him a measure of balm, for Jeffries grew so engrossed in his subject that he forgot to mention Catherine, and completely spared his guest the probing of mundane things.

'Well, there it is,' he said at last. 'Enjoy all you can in Crigga, but tread sensibly – now you know what it's all about.' He would have gone on, but at that moment Clements arrived to hand him a letter, which he accepted grudgingly, scanned impatiently, and threw aside with a grunt. 'Damn,' he growled explosively. 'Damn.' He flung the letter down as though it was an adder, that had nipped him in the grass. 'My boy, the fates are against us. I must get back to London tomorrow on the midday train. Can I leave you to Clements and Shaddy, eh? Just a couple of days. Sorry, old boy, damned annoyed. But it just can't be helped. Eh?'

With features arranged in sympathetic disappointment, Philip soberly agreed. Secretly, he welcomed the opportunity of making the first exploration of Crigga alone – to wander and wonder along the cliffs and by the questing sea, for there was poetry in it. Besides which, there was something else to which he dared not give a name but, which for all Jeffries' parading of spectres from the past, was haunting him still from yesterday's arrival and journey to the house.

QUEST

Next morning the sunshine glittered with shamefaced apology from cliffs smooth and green-headed from the rain. Yesterday's breakers were subsiding into a long swell and, from the window, Philip saw the watchers were already out scanning the bay.

He went downstairs. On the breakfast room sideboard lay two envelopes, one addressed to him, the other for Jeffries – both in Catherine's handwriting. Why she should write so soon to either puzzled him mildly, since the visit had barely begun and he had already conveyed what personal messages there were. He opened his own letter – a page or two of domestic trivia, and an announcement that she had decided to lock up the house and spend the time with her sister, who lived near them in Belgravia. *'I trust that you will find rest and improve health during your stay in Crigga, and be able to do some useful work on your return,'* it concluded, *'Affectionately, Catherine.'*

Dear Catherine. Correct and conventionally fond, meaning so well, yet who invariably spoke about his writing as though it was akin to a mechanical exercise. He turned to see Clements entering, neatly aproned and bonneted, bearing a breakfast tray and a message from Jeffries.

'Master's apologies. He did leave by the earlier train, but do 'ee make yourself comfortable and have the run of the house till he do come back.'

Breakfast completed, he found himself wondering again about Catherine's letter to Jeffries. He picked up the letter curiously and noticed that it had been slit along the top and the enclosure removed. He speculated whether by any chance the contents had some bearing on

Jeffries' earlier departure, though this seemed improbable. Nevertheless, the letters with their sober face of reality blunted the keen edge of his earlier pleasure. In a tinge of depression, he turned to go, and it was in that moment that the strange feeling of other-worldliness came to him.

The breakfast room was situated in the relatively isolated north wing of the house. He was quite alone, and suddenly everything was bathed in an eerie stillness. It was a strangely tense silence, of the kind one might sense in an unhallowed place, and it began seeping into his consciousness like a vapour penetrating his nerve-ends and petrifying his will.

Instinctively, Philip turned. The emanation grew stronger and seemed to be flowing from a door at the far end of the room. He stared entranced, and it was as though invisible fingers were beckoning – urging him to come. Slowly, he crossed to the door. For a moment he tried to resist the compulsion, then reached for the handle and opened it. Within was a small room bearing evidence of neglect. From it another door half open, led into an equally deserted conservatory – the latter little more than a stoutly-constructed lean-to. In it were a few house plants, an old table or two, and a massively padlocked trapdoor set in the middle of the planked flooring.

It all seemed innocuous enough, but the sensation of being held in suspension increased, poised on the brink of deeper awareness of things that were past and yet to be. It persisted until gradually the conservatory shimmered with a vibratory presence, and from its core, as he stood transfixed, the outlines of human features began slowly to form. They were ghostly, wavering in depth as if in reflection from a rippling pool, yet sufficiently clear to suggest he was looking on the face of Sara Michal, or someone miraculously like her. For a moment she gazed on him – eyes pleading, lips helplessly striving to articulate a cry – then quickly receded, as though being drawn back into a bottomless pit of the unknown.

He shivered in the close air, and instinctively stepped back into the inner room. It was not until he had done so that he noticed for the first time the picture hanging in the far dim corner.It was an old painting, one that appeared to have been hung there out of the way. It was a scene portraying the headland, recognisable as it must have been before the intrusion of the Grey House. There were sails on the summer sea in the background, and in the foreground, a young fisher-girl, pensively gazing towards the bay. She could have been Sara Michal, yet it was the same face that had looked upon him in the conservatory. Fascinated, Philip studied the canvas again. In the bottom corner was a small signature: *John Michal, Crigga, 1862.*

Shaddy's voice came from somewhere outside. There were sounds of Clements replying, and suddenly everything was commonplace again. By the time Philip had gathered his wits and retreated outside, he was willing to believe there were two quite rational explanations: either he had been thinking of Sara to such an extent that he had begun to visualise her, or subconsciously he had noticed the painting on the way through to the conservatory and got the images mixed. Yet neither solution satisfied him. The apparition had been too real, the initial compulsion to enter the conservatory too great. Whichever way he twisted his thoughts he was left with imponderables, and the sense of illusion persisted throughout the day.

Clements would make no comment. In the garden he came across Shaddy Bunt. He would have questioned him on the matter and on Crigga lore in general, but the Cornishman seemed unnaturally wary of him, and in any case was undisposed towards gossiping on equal terms with 'they furriners from Lunnon.' Philip went his way, perplexed, determining to tackle Jeffries on his return.

For the rest of the day, he wandered the seaward enchantments of Crigga, standing dizzily on the furthest cliffs, exploring the ruined mass of the abandoned harbour, venturing into the confines of the quay. The fish had not yet come, but come they must, and the air was vibrating with growing tension. Watchers were strung along every vantage point, searching the sea for the errant pilchards, greybeards manning the huer's hut, from which they would direct the boats when the shoals arrived. Philip kept to himself, though questioning glances were flung at him, and he overheard many murmurings against the grey house. Once, as he tentatively picked his way across the rocks beyond the quay jetty, a fisherman warned: 'Do 'ee take care, mister. Tide'll get 'ee, else.' And another responded: 'Good riddance to 'ee, then!'

Several dinghies were now active, and in one of them he caught sight of Pendenna and old Pemberthy. Joe was skilfully sculling the little craft. Suddenly, with telepathic awareness, he glanced up, and the two men stared stonily at each other. Then Pendenna turned back and the boat glided beyond the harbour wall.

Tired but still restless, Philip roamed again in the evening. In pensive mood he returned to the cliffs above the harbour, where in a nook above the fish cellars, he discovered a rough bench hewn into the rock. Dusk was approaching, once more the disconsolate groups were beginning to break up and melancholy prevailed. He sat for a while, lulled by the lap of the now flooding tide, pondering the frustrations of life.

Somewhere out there, following their instinctive ways, entirely unaware of their role in the Crigga drama, millions of pilchards were gathering. On shore, in readiness with equipment, knowledge and technique perfected over generations of experience, hundreds of people waited for the fish to shoal in.

All the fish had to do was to turn shoreward and the process would swing into instant motion. Until they did, each link in the vital organisation was useless, the whole of Crigga overshadowed by fears, worries, accumulating stress and strains. It would be alright when the fish came. But suppose just for once they failed to turn. And if failing to turn, there was little the most hopeful struggler could do about it.

He rose to go, and it was then that he saw the book – a slim volume that had apparently fallen from the side of the bench and was resting in a hollow on the rough ground. It looked vaguely familiar. He picked it up, inspecting it more closely, and now he felt the place really must be bewitched, for the title read: *The Wickenham Book of Verse* – his own introductory book of poetry, published a year ago. Of all objects on a remote Cornish cliffside – surely this was the most unlikely for him to find! The book had been well-used. Intrigued, he opened it. On the flyleaf was written in a firm, intelligent hand: *'To Sara Michal. Teignmouth, 1881. With blessings from John.'* And underneath, in more delicate characters: *'Sara Michal, 1881.'* Pemberthy's granddaughter, and a link with his own poetry – in this deserted place? He closed the book slowly, with, as another poet had said: '*A strange wonder, potently fed* …' He looked up to see Sara making her way up the rough track towards him.

Both were startled, frozen in momentary surprise. Sara looked widely at Philip, at the ground by the seat, and finally at the book in his hand. For a while he could only stare at her, held by her dainty beauty, so out of place against the workaday canvas of Crigga. He was again amazed at the likeness to the girl in the painting. Her hair was blown across her face, a shawl lightly hung from her shoulders and she was dressed for the toil she had been attempting, but she retained a dignity and quiet poise that was compelling. The clean air and sunshine had coaxed a streak of colour to her cheeks, though there was still a solemn depth in her eyes.

'Your book, I believe,' Wickenham ventured at last.

She looked at him gravely, 'Thank you. I was stupid to leave it there. It would have been awful to lose it.'

'Yes,' Philip said, 'I'm glad you didn't.' He proffered the book, which she took with the faintest of smiles. 'You are fond of reading?'

'Whenever I can.' She glanced back down the pathway, not entirely at ease. 'I didn't thank you properly for helping me at the station. It was so kind of you.'

'It was nothing. I'm glad that you are so much better. The journey must have been terribly trying.'

'Yes, but it wasn't only the journey. I had had a very long day.' She gazed down the pathway again, as though expecting to see someone. 'Thank you again for finding the book.' She smiled and added hastily, 'but I don't even know your name.'

'You may call me Philip.'

'Oh – and now I really must go.' She turned with reluctance.

He hesitated for a moment, then, on an impulse, 'Sara,' he said.

'Yes?'

'Forgive the suddenness. But since you are in a hurry to go?' He paused, searching for the right approach. 'I would like to talk more with you – about yourself…'

She met his eyes frankly, 'I think I would like that, too. But it would be difficult. You can't imagine how difficult.'

Memories of the last three days fresh in his mind,

Philip smiled wryly. 'Perhaps I can. But a talk would be harmless enough. Surely something could be arranged?' He waited for her reply.

She moved from the centre of the path into the shielding angle of the cliff face, then gestured towards the fish cellars and the quay. 'I should like to talk with you,' she said honestly, 'but how to explain? You come from the grey house. There is so much difference between us, and so many people watching.'

'Your grandparents? Joe Pendenna?'

'Not only them. Everybody. It's like a whole different world.'

'To which *you* don't belong,' he was tempted to say, but checked at the fleeting pain on her face. 'I'm sorry,' he said, 'I'm embarrassing you. But I will come here most evenings and wait by this seat. And if by chance you are able ...'

Sara shook her head, doubtfully, 'I wouldn't be able, and it would be unwise to come here.' She hesitated, as though at odds with herself, and then suddenly her face lit with a mere wraith of a smile. 'I *should* like to talk,' she repeated, 'if only to believe again that there *was* something else in the world beside fish.'

'And there is,' Wickenham assured her.

'Well,' she said doubtfully, 'there *is* another place, above this, overlooking the big cove.'

'I will find it,' he promised.

'But not if the fish come – and not tomorrow,' she said quickly, 'I'm going to Pennan tomorrow – *if* the fish allow.'

'Pennan? Where's that?'

'It's a village the other side of the west headland.'

'Is it far?'

'I suppose about two or three miles – if the tide is right.'

'And you are going alone?'

'Yes.' She paused. 'Joe was to have taken me, but he must stand by the boats.'

'Then,' said Philip, 'is there any reason why I should not walk with you to Pennan?'

'Oh, you must not, you really must not. Please, I must hurry back now.' She drew the shawl round her shoulders and stepped away from the cliff.

'Please,' Philip answered, 'why should I not walk with you?'

'No, it is impossible. Please, you must understand.' She turned and began to walk down the path, leaving him desolate. Then, as she reached the corner, she swung round and looked at him anxiously, 'There is an old ruined harbour – at the foot of the other side of the headland. They do not watch for the pilchards there. I shall be there tomorrow at about ten o'clock.'

Within seconds she was out of sight, clutching her precious book, and it was only then that he opened his mind fully to the simple truth it had striven to reject all day – that his aimless wanderings had concealed a deeper quest. Crigga with all its charms and magnificence had entranced and intrigued him, but the true search, illogical, hopeless, disastrously unwise, had been for Sara Michal alone.

SARA MICHAEL'S STORY

Wickenham's conscience brought him no solace that night. Despite the deep feeling he now had for Sara, and which he no longer fought to resist, the futility of the proposed meeting became increasingly obvious to him. The obvious logic pointed only at the certainty of eventual disaster to Sara, Catherine and everyone concerned – unless he broke free from the spell that was entrancing him. Secretly to acknowledge this fatal attraction to Sara was one thing – attempting to consummate it, unthinkable. Yet still his mind wavered, a torn battleground between the possible and impossible, the sterile hope and the unattainable dream.

By the time the dawn peeped mockingly through the open window he had reached an inspired compromise – he would meet Sara, fulfilling part of his promise, but not accompany her all the way to Pennan. Thus, all aspects of conscience might be satisfied without further harm being done.

This fragile resolve bolstered him through breakfast and a subsequent exchange on the prospect of the pilchards with Shaddy, only to vaporise utterly the moment Sara came into sight on the old harbour path carrying a heavy basket. The basket, he assured himself, completely altered the case, for no gentleman with any pretentions to chivalry, at that time, could allow a young lady to struggle with such a load the whole distance to Pennan. There was some truth in this, and for the first part of the walk the delusion kept pace with him, till the peace of the day and the natural rapport between them made excuses useless.

In their newfound companionship, neither noticed that Shadrach – burningly curious at Philip's movements –

had followed him and was now watching them out of sight from the dunes.

The basket was certainly lumpy. It held – Sara explained – salted fish and other items from the Pemberthys for her grandmother's sister, Mrs Curnow of Pennan, in return for which she was to bring cream, butter and eggs from the relatives. It was a weekly transaction, and once the pilchard harvest was gathered there would be no question of her making the journey alone. Even today, she said, there were doubts about letting her go, but surely the fish must arrive at any moment, and neither Pemberthy nor Pendenna could be spared – being key to the business of netting the shoals.

'Joe – is he a relative?' asked Philip.

'No, just a friend of the family. They own a boat together, that's all.'

'That's all?'

'Well, Joe's people are dead, so grandmother cooks for him – and things like that.'

'He's not married, then?'

'No.' she said, shortly.

'Does he live with the Pemberthys?'

'Oh, no – his cottage is down on the quayside.'

They walked for a while without speaking, approaching the western bay. To Philip's mind the pattern was becoming miserably clear and his thoughts traced a dismal linkage – a bachelor without parents, a young attractive girl without parents, a waiting cottage … He forced his imagination to halt before the picture completely unrolled, remembering his resolution. And Sara was different. She didn't fit into set pieces as simply as that.

The silence prevailed until they had skirted the foreshore and were nearing the western headland, its bleak mass ominous even on this glorious day. The sun was now blazing, but across this exposed stretch of coastline there was a constant breeze and, whatever sea-moods the weather allowed on the Crigga side, here the rollers growled and thundered incessantly, sending fierce eddies of spume across the broad beach. There was no road, no cliff – except the towering shambles of sand tufted with dune grass.

'I'm afraid I've been asking too many questions,' he said, eventually. And for the first time Sara smiled.

'Well, if we're really going to get to know one another...'

The rest of the sentence faded into the wind, but he thought it ended, 'and I don't even know your name.'

For a moment he let that pass, more than content to watch her walking a little in front of him, head back, hair tossed in the wind, lips parted as though kissing back the sun's caress.

'You've been to Pennan before?' he asked.

'I can't remember. I've only been here once when I was a tiny child. And you?'

'No, I've never been to Crigga before.'

'You're from the grey house, aren't you? I think it's what the locals call Greywalls.'

'Just visiting.'

She sighed. 'And now in the eyes of the world I'm a Crigga girl. We're absolute opposites. We shouldn't be together, you know.'

Again, he was intrigued by the quality of her voice, the clear evidence of culture.

'In the eyes of the world,' he prompted.

She looked rather bleakly at him. 'But you must have wondered? The way I arrived, all that tension.'

'It was no business of mine.'

'But you wondered? You must have done.'

'I am still wondering.' He tried to seem noncommittal, as though questions had not been fermenting in his mind. But she seemed willing to talk.

'Nobody has told you?' she asked, and Philip was glad when she continued without pressing for a reply. 'No, Crigga folk don't confide in strangers, and they wouldn't know much up at the grey house. But I'm going to tell you.' She fixed her gaze on him, then: 'I'm the Crigga scandal – the return of the bastard child.'

Her voice was forcedly even, but tense. Philip was silent, wholly sympathetic, thankful she had been so ready to confide.

'You are shocked?' Sara asked.

'No,' he said, sincerely, 'I'm trying to understand.'

'That,' said Sara, 'would mean more to me than anything. Ever since I came, I've been longing to talk to someone. But it's all fish and accusing looks. It's a different world.'

Philip sought for and fleetingly touched her hand. 'You need not say anything. But if it would help at all ...'

'Oh, it would.'

'Then why have you come? What of your parents?' He could have whipped his tongue at the sudden pain on her face.

'They are dead,' she told him, quietly.

'Oh, I am so sorry.'

'Please, you must not be. Why else should I have come alone to Crigga?' She looked at him with the wide, honest gaze he found so disconcerting. 'My father and Alicia – a wonderful woman who helped to bring me up – were lately drowned in a boating accident, and – I'm sorry.' She could not continue.

'I'm so sorry ...'

'Shall we stop for a while?' she asked at length, 'We've a steep climb ahead of us.'

They sat in a hollow of the dunes with the first slopes

of the western headland looming above them.

'We have to go up and over that,' said Sara. She opened the basket. 'Grandmother put a pasty in here for my lunch. Would you like to share it?'

The pasty was appetising, the sand warm, the atmosphere contented. After a while she turned to him with a naturalness that could have been born from a lifetime of intimacy.

'I'm glad I can talk to you. I want you to know – in case other people – I want you to know the truth.'

'Then tell me.'

She smiled wryly. 'But where do I begin? So much of it happened before I was born. Mother ran away from Crigga with my father … That was the scandal. They were never married.'

While the gulls wheeled expectantly for crumbs and the heat shimmered rhythmically from the sand, she told him the story as far as she knew it. How a generation ago, John Michal had come to Crigga to paint, how he had fallen in love with Ruth Pemberthy, and they had eloped. How, on a mysterious visit to Crigga when Sara was little more than a year old, Ruth had been killed in a mysterious storm. 'Somehow, as young as I was, I remember it,' Sara shuddered, 'All the crashing noise and screaming … Then Father took me away … He and Alicia brought me up … He had a little studio in Teignmouth then … and …' She turned away, grief welling in her eyes again. 'They were drowned – in the boat. And afterwards I thought – I thought of Crigga.'

'You thought Crigga was the only place to come?' Philip asked.

At last, the whole Crigga tragedy was taking shape in his consciousness, and he felt deeply for Sara, on whom the effects of bereavement, travel, and the almost hostile reception, must have been devastating.

'Yes,' she said in a whisper, 'but I didn't really know – Father had told me so little. But I felt, somehow, he wanted to make his peace with Crigga, and there was little money, nowhere else I could go. But I didn't know that, after all this time, they still haven't forgiven.'

'But they knew you were coming?'

'I wrote to them. I didn't realise that neither Grandfather nor Grandmother could read or write, and that by the time they had got someone to do it for them, it was too late for a reply. You know the rest, how I arrived and what happened. Now I must be patient and make the best of it. There is nothing else I can do.' She smiled weakly at him. 'Well, now you know all that I know.'

'Things are very bad?' Wickenham asked.

'In some ways. They have accepted me, if only on sufferance, and Grandfather tries to be kind. Grandmother – I didn't know …'

'What?'

For the first time her voice trembled with fear. 'She is strange, she won't speak to me. She's in a half-trance most of the time. She keeps muttering about – about babbies, and death and disaster to come through a third stranger. It frightens me sometimes. I try to keep out of her way.'

'The third stranger?' Their eyes met fleetingly, and Philip felt a quiver run through him. It was all so much on the Crigga pattern of lurking bewitchment. Neither spoke, but the thought stole each of them: Jeffries, John Michal, Philip himself. Three. John Michal dead, Jeffries inextricably bound in the Crigga coils, Philip already sensing the tightening noose. Could he in fact be the mysterious visitant haunting the tortured old woman's mind? And what lay behind the threat implied in the constant muttering? It was Sara who broke the silence.

'You see how it is between you and I? If they could

see us now? What they might think or do?'

Philip saw. Clearly all Crigga knew of this tragic tale, held it in shocked and resentful remembrance, and would read an ominous significance in Sara's contact with him – however innocent. He made a belated attempt to correct his folly.

'It mustn't come to that,' he said, seriously, 'For your sake, perhaps I had better go.'

'No!' she said, with such urgency that his heart thrilled and resolution evaporated like a tide-lap in the sand. 'It is only once. Forget the troubles, if only for a day. Talk about something else.'

It was difficult to change the subject completely. 'Your father,' he asked at length, recalling the inner room at Greywalls, 'If he was *John* Michal…'

'Yes.'

'Well, there's a painting by him at Greywalls.'

'Really?' Sara was thrilled. 'Well, of course, he sold a few.'

'This,' Philip said carefully, 'is of the headland – before the Greywalls was built. There's a fisher-girl in it. At first, I thought it was you. But, of course, it can't have been.'

'Oh,' For a moment Sara was puzzled, then again, their gaze became joined in a common interpretation. 'Mother!' she breathed.

'I think so. She is very like you …' He paused, for Sara was visibly moved. 'Jeffries – my host – could have met your mother. He almost certainly came across your father.'

'And now I've met you. How strange,' she said, wistfully. 'So long ago, and all this coming together again. Do you know, I somehow feel closer to Greywalls than to my family.' She turned to him with a sudden eagerness. 'Perhaps he – Mr. Jeffries – knows what really happened?'

'It is possible. I will ask. When exactly did your mother die?'

'Oh, I know that. Father always kept the anniversary. It was September 15th, 1864. The night of the great storm.'

'Then Greywalls was just about built. Yes, I will certainly ask him. Unless you would rather not know.'

'Oh, please. I *do* want to know.'

'And your people here have really told you nothing?'

'Nothing – except that the misfortune came from the grey house.'

Wickenham shook his head, bewildered. 'But Greywalls couldn't have been responsible for the storm that killed your mother.'

'They do say so. I don't understand it either, but it's no use trying. Grandmother never answers, the others evade. Father would never speak of it. As far as I know, there wasn't a grave. So, you see …' She stared pensively out to sea, a perfect replica of the girl in the painting. 'I've a feeling, now, that Father would want me to know.'

'I will do what I can,' he promised, though with little hope of Jeffries indulging in such an enquiry. Then, gently, 'Tell me, what was your father like?'

'Beautiful.' Impulsively, she turned back to him, a smile lighting her face again. 'That sounds strange to you – calling a man beautiful? But he was – a beautiful, beautiful man.'

Pleased at the change of mood, he couldn't help smiling at her. 'Alright, Sara Michal, I believe you. But what sort of a person *was* he?'

She looked at him directly, eyes suddenly agleam with the vivacity of a child. 'Well – of course, he was artistic, sensitive, understanding – a little intolerant. But not quite so quiet.' She nodded, pleased with her assessment.

'Ah. And was he very old?'

'Daddy wasn't old. He could never be old. What have years got to do with it?' She was uncompromising, positive. 'Look at the sea and the cliffs. They're centuries old, but they're always lovely.'

Lifted by her enthusiasm, Wickenham laughed. 'Then we've a few years to go. I shall probably end up a real old man of the sea.'

'We must go,' Sara told him, regretfully.

'I suppose we must, if we're going to beat that tide.'

'Just five minutes more,' Sara urged.

They relaxed side by side by the grasses, now completely at ease with each other – barriers down. Everything was very peaceful, with no sound – except for the muffled beat of the sea. Even the gulls had gone silent. A tiny grain glinted among the brown sand, sparkling as the sun caught it and danced with it. And always afterwards it glowed in Philip's poetic mind as an emblem of those precious moments – a golden gleam, shining out, soon to be scuffed in the sand.

'It's so wonderfully *quiet*,' sighed Sara, and Philip was tempted to quote: '… where spectres haunt the unbent grass, and no bird sings …'

'Mourn,' Sara murmured, sleepily.

'What?' Philip asked, surprised.

'Where spectres *mourn* the unbent grass, and no bird sings – not haunt. Mourn makes all the difference if you read the poem. It's in my book.'

'Is it indeed?' Wickenham said, amused. 'Well, it's in mine, too. But I may be wrong.'

'Oh, you *are* wrong,' she said, 'I've read the poem again and again. It's about renunciation: Yes, you may go. Then there will be no music, no song … So, the spectres mourn, not haunt.'

'I see,' said Wickenham, 'I'll have to look up the

verse again.'

'Do you like poetry? I thought you might.'

'Well, sometimes. Just some of it.'

'Well, do you like Wickenham's?' She stirred dreamily. 'The ones in my book?'

Wickenham paused, moved by the piquancy of the situation. 'Honestly,' he answered ironically, 'I'm not qualified to give an opinion.'

'Oh, I think you would,' she chatted on drowsily, 'but he's a sad man, you know. Terribly, terribly sad.'

'Good lord, do you honestly think so?'

'Well, most of his poems are, and the poems reflect the poet. Wouldn't you say? To me he's like a man in the wilderness, searching, searching in sorrow.'

He was intrigued. 'And what is he searching for, Sara?'

Her eyes were closed. She spoke softly, so dreamily she could have been asleep. 'I don't really know – a lost truth, a love, or a love not yet found. How could any man write poems like Renunciation without having suffered a lot?'

'*Suffering*?' Wickenham repeated, 'Is that what you really believe?'

'Oh, yes,' she said, 'Suffering. Suffering in the mind. Perhaps suffering he knows is yet to be. Why else should he write: '...*To hold you, hurry by the place where Heaven weeps/Lest broken vows turn all our tender dreams to stone?*' She drifted into silence, then:

Where tears have been, heartache and pain, let these atone –

Bring back to waking bloom the bud that gently sleeps.

Dear God, whose bounteous fingers hold all love, each promised thing.

Grant me but this: if love I must, let me not walk alone.

Her voice had fallen almost to a whisper, 'Oh, people shouldn't write things like that,' she said half ashamed of herself, 'They make me cry.' Yet she had read the extract beautifully and with a deep response.

Wickenham, himself, was on the delicate borderline between laughter and tears, 'Then why do you read them, Sara?'

She sat up, smiling suddenly, 'Because I like them. And because sometimes women like a good cry. Didn't you know that?' She gestured towards the headland as a sign that they had lingered enough, and he was glad she hadn't looked too closely into his face. 'Wickenham knew,' she said positively, 'I'm sure he's the most marvellous man.'

PENNAN

They toiled up the slope and over the headland brow into a new wonderland. Below lay the estuary, long and wide, and at low tide a wilderness of reed and sand transformed the flood into a mighty lake.

From the headland shoulder the river seemed a mere runnel snaking its way to the sea. To the south west yet another promontory thrust its dark limb from a shoreline similar to the one that lay behind them. The opposite bank of the river mouth reared from a jigsaw of inlets to smooth stretches of pastureland crested by trees.

'It's devilish hard going,' puffed Wickenham.

Sara laughed. 'No more resting,' she said, 'There's the bridge, and Pennan is right over there.'

A high narrow lane wound down to the river, flanked by high hedges which grew lusher as the road descended. Here, there was a complete screening from the wind, and the air was rich with the scent of wildflowers and the monotone of bees. Soon they emerged on the flat fringing rocks of the estuary and picked their way around the pools to the river itself.

The bridge barely qualified for the title, being merely a contraption of barnacle-encrusted planks below which, at low water, the stream was reduced to a few lazy trickles. Having crossed it, a further network of streams had to be negotiated, and it was some time before Sara and Philip came near to the further bank. On this side an inviting prospect of smooth shore held the hidden menace of quicksand, sucking feet down to ankle depth as they crossed. At last, exhausted, they struggled to firmer ground and came to a breathless halt.

'Not far now,' said Sara, consulting a roughly drawn map, 'but we'd better not dawdle.'

Wickenham looked around. From the low-lying spot the sea seemed an impossible distance away, and it was hard to imagine that it could ever advance enough to flood this wide valley. But there was evidence here that it did, for the cliff face was nibbled by a series of creeks showing high water marks and dotted by salt-water pools.

'Where now?' he asked, and Sara pointed.

They plodded towards the shore till she indicated the last of the inlets, broad and fronted with sandhills. Gradually, these funnelled into a country lane, half a mile along which Pennan lay cradled among trees, the squat church hunching its tower over the hedge tops.

Wickenham slowed. It would be unwise for them to be seen in the village together. Sara looked at him, sensing his thoughts.

'It's too late now. We've probably been spotted already.'

'I was only thinking of you.'

'Pennan folk won't talk, at least not to Crigga folk. There's a long-standing feud between them. Till lately, even the Pemberthys and Curnows wouldn't speak to each other. The news might get back, but by then …' she added with a tinge of regret, 'All this will be over.'

Near the old vicarage, set on a sheltered slope on the edge of the village, a dog padded out to pass the time of day. It was the first sign of domestic life they had seen since leaving Crigga. He circled his tail amiably, watching them round the turn to the church with lazy curiosity.

The parson, a small, plump figure in cassock and biretta, had just come through the ancient lych-gate. Strangers were practically unknown in Pennan, and he waited to have a word with them as they went by.

'Ah, come to call on the Curnows, then, have you?' he asked, when, after the first polite exchanges, Sara mentioned her destination. He glanced keenly at her, then closely at Philip, bubbling with refined inquisitiveness. The Pemberthy story was well known in Pennan and, as Vicar, he was as familiar with the background as the inhabitants of church or chapel. 'Pity you can't stay longer. Should like to show you the church. Wonderful old place, this. Steeped in history. Legend has it there was once a thriving town here, you know – centuries ago – swallowed up by the sand. Before my time, eh?' he chuckled. 'Ah, well, God works in a mysterious way … Yes, should like to show you the church. We've got the old stocks, you know, and quite a fine window. Some other time, perhaps? You'll be over at Pennan again?' The well-meaning clerical prattle flowed smoothly till Sara eventually broke in.

'Thank you, Vicar, but we really must be on our way.'

'Why, certainly my dear, certainly. We *do* ramble on, you know. Wouldn't dream of detaining you. Give my regards to your aunt. Ah – am I right? Mrs. Curnow *is* your aunt? You great aunt, should it be? You *are* Sara Pemberthy? From Crigga? Hm, hm?'

'Sara Michal,' Sara corrected, and wished him a solemn good day. 'You see?' she said to Wickenham as they walked away, 'everyone knows everything here.'

'Perhaps I should look at the church when you go to see your aunt?'

'No. It would be strange if you left me now and we met again later. I'd rather be open about it.'

Pennan, that afternoon, was loaded with trapped summer, its gardens exotic with colour – the hedges and trees vocal with bird mutterings and the lazy whisperings of insects. Sara led the way past a granite-enclosed well at the village centre, and on towards an ancient inn – still vibrant with the departed shades of smugglers. An elderly man, leaning beside the gate of a nearby cottage, could well be the reincarnation of one of them.

'If my directions are right,' Sara murmured, 'that's the place – and that must be my great uncle Sam.'

The figure by the gate roused and came towards them. Over the years, Sam Curnow had slumped rather than mellowed. Fat ran in horizontal runnels under his chin, and his fisherman's jersey did little to hide a well-endowed paunch. But his eyes still shot darkly from his weather eroded face. Patches of grey suddenly shaded it as he stared at Sara.

'God save us, who be this, then?'

'I'm Sara from Crigga.'

'Sara, ezza?' He swept sweaty beads from his brow with a broad forearm. 'Dear souls, I did think … What's to do, then? You be the Pemberthy's maid?'

'Well, their granddaughter.'

'Ess, we did hear 'ee were coming. Where be Luke and they others? Still waiting cry, ezza?'

'Yes, still waiting.'

'Ess, ess.' Sam had recovered himself and placed a great hand on her arm. 'How don't they fish come, eh?' He turned to Wickenham sharply. 'Who be this, then, maid?' She felt the grip on her arm tighten.

Sara looked at Philip, suddenly struck by the absurdity that in all this time he had not mentioned his name.

'Just call me Philip.'

'This gentleman was kind enough …' she began, but already Sam was waving them down in a flurry of grunted Cornish.

'Best 'ee be careful, maid. Don't 'ee know about strangers? Godsakes, ent there trouble enough? But good or bad, cums 'ee in and see missus, else she be vexed. And there be milk and some heavy cake too, if 'ee likes …'

After the first shock, Rachel's reception was warily

hospitable. She had little tolerance for the weaknesses of the world and looked upon Philip with unspoken suspicion. Ruth's tragic dilemma and death remained a scar on her memory. She was too near her sister in tradition and temperament not to feel involvement in the family scandal. 'How did 'ee bring *he*, then?' she demanded in a fierce whisper, as Philip lingered in embarrassment on the pathway.

'He helped me carry the basket.'

'And Grandmother knows of 'un?'

'Not yet. He met me along the way.'

'Don't 'ee make trouble, maid ...'

Sam settled the issue with his usual forthrightness, 'Aw, best cums along in, mister. Sit 'ee down, both of 'ee. How don't 'ee bring 'un some milk and a saffern bun then, missus?'

'I'll help you,' said Sara.

'No, sit 'ee down, maid.' Ignoring Philip, Sam indicated the wooden settle by the hearth. He sank into a chair, produced a rope of ship's tobacco, and began whittling. 'Do 'ee tell us what news there be from Crigga.'

'I don't know much. This is only my second full day.'

'Ess, ess. Must be strange for 'ee, maid, and in truth, I never thought to see 'ee again.'

'So – you've seen me before?'

'Ess, if seeing the babby be seeing the maid,' Curnow grunted, 'It were the day that your mammy died – no thanks to the stranger.'

'The day that she died?' Sara tensed. 'The night of the storm?'

'Storm? Storm?' he shrugged, 'Ess, if that's what the Crigga folk *call* a storm.'

'Tell me,' Sara urged, 'What happened – exactly? How did my mother die?'

48

Sam shook his head firmly, 'It were an accident,' he said, 'long ago. Ent no place of mine to gossip on Crigga troubles. Best forgotten, maid.' He would say no more.

Wickenham had relaxed in a window-seat while they talked, welcoming the peace of the little parlour.

There was a blend of sound from the voices, an occasional clink of pots from the kitchen, the wheezy tick of a clock, and the yawning chirrup of birds from the thatch. Suddenly, Sam turned to him.

'Do 'ee smoke then, mister?' A handful of roughly-shredded tobacco was being held towards him. He declined with thanks. 'Ah, you be one of they cigar puffers, then?'

'Not really, no.'

Sam crammed his pipe, lit it, and exuded a thick cloud of acridity across the room. 'Keep they darned flies way. So 'ee cummed over from Crigga? Where from? You ent from Cornwall,' he noted with an edge of suspicion.

'Actually, I come from London.'

'How do 'ee like Cornwall? Not a-feared o' they piskies, then?'

'No. Should I be?'

'Ahh, they'll get 'ee proper mazed, they piskies, and watch out that the crake don't get 'ee. Where did 'ee meet up with the maid?'

'On the headland,' said Wickenham, not specifying which one.

Curnow eyed him shrewdly, continuing the interrogation with bluff directness. For Sara's sake, Philip answered as patiently as he could.

'Were 'ee coming to Pennan, then?'

'Yes, it seemed the day for it.'

'Tes always the day for Pennan, boy. What do 'ee do for a living, then? Don't catch they fish, do 'ee, now?'

'Nothing so adventurous, I'm afraid.'

'Afraid? Afraid? What be the use of that? What *do* 'ee do, then?'

Wickenham sensed Sara's gaze on him and dare not meet it. 'As a matter of fact,' he said casually, 'I make a living by writing.'

'Writing?' Sam chuckled in earthy amusement, 'Writing? What use be that to man or beast?'

Philip, smiling, struck mildly back. 'Some people profit from it, and some don't,' he said easily, 'As to the beasts, I've never bothered to ask them.'

'Eh, boy?' Sam puffed his pipe. Then: 'Tell us then, mister, what be the name?'

'Philip,' he said, briefly.

'Ess, ess, 'ee told me that. What else then, mister?'

'Wickenham.'

There was a sharp breath from Sara, but Sam pressed on regardless.

'Be 'ee married, then?'

Again, Philip hesitated. The inquisition was cruel.

'Yes.'

'Babbies?'

'No.'

'How ent the missus with 'ee, then?'

'She prefers London,' Wickenham said shortly.

He glanced towards Sara at last. She stared back – her face mottled with red. Before anything more could be said, Rachel re-entered, bearing a pitcher of milk, cups, and thick slices of saffron cake. She served them with restrained courtesy, speaking only when necessary, avoiding conversation with Wickenham. Sam chattered on with bland insensitivity – between huge mouthfuls of cake and pulls at his smouldering pipe. Philip went through the motions of eating and drinking in prickly unhappiness, and was glad when, eventually, Sam looked over to Sara.

'You'm to catch that old tide, maid. Crake'll get 'ee, else.' He stood up. 'Cums along now, missus. Where be that basket? Mind 'ee now, mister, don't 'ee go breaking they eggs.'

When the woman had disappeared in search of the basket, he took Wickenham aside.

'Like Cornwall, do 'ee?'

'Yes, very much.'

'Had a good day, 'ave 'ee, over to Pennan?'

'Excellent, thanks.'

'Ess,' said Sam, thoughtfully, 'ess, I do expect 'ee have – and better than 'ee deserves.' He prodded Philip firmly with the stem of his pipe. 'Get 'ee back to that Lunnon, then, as soon as 'ee likes. Us never looks to see 'ee again, mind, not in Pennan nor Crigga. Ent no place down-along here for the likes of 'ee.' The stem ground harder into Wickenham's ribs. 'And do 'ee keep clear o' the maid.'

BARRIERS

Both Sara and Philip were pensive as they made their way back past the church and into the lane. His thoughts revolved mainly around Sam Curnow who, despite his bluff hospitality, had crystallised and made articulate the animosities of both Pennan and Crigga. The words of the fisherman were the essence of warning against Greywalls, against the stranger who had upset the rhythm of the shoals, against the man who had revivified the memories of Ruth Pemberthy's fall and – above all – a warning to leave Sara Michal alone. Her musing had been more personalised.

'You might have told me – the name, I mean.'

'I should have,' he agreed, guiltily, 'But it was desperately difficult. And so absurd. How *could* I have interrupted you and said, "Hold on a moment. *I'm* Philip Wickenham. It was I who wrote those poems!" You would have thought I was joking.' He sought her hand. 'Besides, you were reading the extracts so beautifully.'

'But all the things I said.'

'A writer must be prepared for interpretation. And they were nice things. And now you know.'

She stopped and turned to him, a deeply grave look in her eyes. 'But I *don't* know. I know that you're married, that you have no children, that your wife lives in London, that she doesn't like the sea …'

'All that should be enough,' he said, soberly, striving not to match the rising plea in her tone.

'But it *isn't* enough. Not for me, not for either of us. I want to know the Philip of the poems, the inspiring, sensitive man. Is it true what I thought? *Have* you suffered? *Are* you searching? And for what?'

He resisted the bait. 'That man is too tangled up with

the other. It's a hopeless task.'

'No,' she insisted, 'not hopeless. Exciting. Oh, I've wondered about you ever since Father first showed me the poems. I can't believe that I've actually met you, that I'm with you now.'

They strolled for a while in silence.

'The poems,' Sara repeated, 'Surely someone or something inspires them.'

'I suppose so – but not just one person or one thing.'

'Your wife?' she quavered.

He had expected this, but the last thing he wanted in those moments was a discussion about Catherine.

'I write to an ideal,' he said, evasively, 'a universal ideal. Catherine is part of that.'

It was a weak defence, and Sara, with feminine directness, outflanked it immediately. 'And do you love her very much?'

'*Please*,' Wickenham begged quietly, and she was at once repentant, though a glance at his profile made her heart quicken, the unspoken answer on his sensitive face plain to see. Fleetingly, his grip on her hand tightened, and they continued in wordless rapport, following the track till it dipped to meet the dunes.

'Philip …' she said in a while.

He stopped as she turned to him. 'Sara?'

'The ideal you spoke of. Could *I* ever be a part of it?'

She stood there, wide-eyed, dainty, bringing him at once to delight and desolation. His whole being shrunk at the irony of it, that after all these years searching for the embodiment of his ideal, his vision, he had only to reach out – yet must not. Words then would have been clumsy, for the truth was defencelessly held in his eyes. She drew nearer. The tension vibrated between them, and both knew that surrender would have erupted at the merest quiver of a kiss. Yet by some miracle the fine thread of reticence held, and it was Philip who, with agonising control, urged her gently from him and encouraged her to resume the walk towards the sea.

'You are wise,' he forced himself to say, 'Don't put too much trust in poetic fancies, or the perfection we glimpse that can never materialise.' And there was nothing more to be said if the entire fabric of his resolution was not to be ripped apart.

Gradually he steered the conversation from poetry to the countryside, to the balm of the approaching evening, and the threatening magic was allowed to drain away from everyday things. It was as well, for in a matter of moments they were tumbled back into the harsh realities from which they had contrived momentarily to escape.

'Oh, God,' he heard Sara breathe faintly, and the throb of anxiety in her voice made him turn to her sharply. '*Look*. Not at me – over *there*.'

They had reached the end of the lane and were topping the rise overlooking the estuary. The tide was in full flood, bringing with it a wind that held fine spray in the air like rain. Through the faint mist the familiar vista of water and scree appeared, smudged now into longer shadows.

'What *is* it?' he pressed, not immediately grasping the significance of the scene. 'I see only cliffs and water.'

'That *is* it,' sighed Sara, 'Only water. The bridge has been covered by the tide.'

Both gazed in horror, realisation of the implications immediate and shattering. Had the tide allowed, they could have parted as they had met at the old harbour. Now, the entire stretch of the long estuary would have to be circumvented with no prospect of arriving at Crigga until after dark. Surely the alarm would be raised and, though no physical coward, Philip cringed at the thought of facing the fisherfolk. The only slight hope was that the cry would go up in the meantime, to concentrate all Crigga's attention elsewhere. Such a hope was slim. Philip gripped Sara's arm and, with desperate optimism, hurried her along the shore towards the crossing place. From the water's edge, the location of the bridge could just be discerned from the eddies swirling around and above its framework. The sea was funnelling relentlessly inland, compressed between the narrow jaws of the river mouth. It was already flowing several inches above the bridge planks, rising at each moment, and spreading – foam licking the containing banks.

'We might just do it,' Philip said, recklessly, 'Wait here, and I'll try it first.'

Ignoring her warning cry, he put down the basket and moved forward – to be retarded by the minor quicksand sucking and tugging at his feet. A few seconds later, the water was up to his ankles, then to his knees as he splashed towards the submerged bridge.

'Come back, it's too dangerous!' Sara pleaded, but something beyond reason seemed to be driving him on, and her cries faded impotently into the wind. He was thigh deep as he reached and struggled to hoist himself to the timbers and, even when he had mounted them, the current was foaming against his knees. The course of the planking was now completely unmarked with an ominous, expanding course of flood water lapping around him. He groped a few steps, bracing himself against the tide. Having managed this far he might have inched slowly to the opposite side, but to make his way back and pilot Sara across was clearly impossible. Yet, still he stood there, as if held by a secret fascination, while the mounting current tore swiftly past him. Sara, tense on the shore, was frantically urging him to return and, when at last he swung round, there was a remote look on his face – oblivious and frightening. 'Come back!' she called helplessly, 'Come back!' And like a sleepwalker suddenly in charge of his senses, he lowered himself reluctantly from the bridge and began the long return to the beach, stumbling towards the foreshore.

Sara found him huddled half in and half out of the water, ominously still. She touched him fearfully, desolate with imaginings. To her great relief, he stirred and opened his eyes. He muttered feebly, and she had to bend low to hear what he was trying to say.

'Tides,' he mumbled, faintly, '*The maelstrom – and you – and you called me back from the shore* …'

The words would haunt her dreams for months to come, but there was no time now for emotion. The flood was still closing in, only yards now from the safety of the bank. Desperately she shook him by the shoulders, urging and willing him to rise.

'Philip, hurry. Listen to me. We can't stay here. Can you manage to get to the cliff?'

From the depths of stupor, he nodded weakly and, with Sara's help, dragged himself from the water and swayed to his feet.

'Will you be alright?' Sara asked, anxiously.

He inclined his head, grey with exhaustion. 'Where do we go from here? Is there another bridge?'

'I don't know.'

'What about the boats?'

'Not now. We shall have to walk all the way round.'

They were silent again, realising what the extra journey meant in terms of the suspicious and hostile Crigga folk.

'I'm sorry,' Wickenham said, humbly, 'I should have thought of these complications before.'

For a moment, she was soft with tenderness, longing to comfort and lovingly scold. Then her pent-up feeling erupted and her eyes flashed with sudden passion. 'Why did you do it? Why did you have to go in the *sea*?'

He turned with a prickled weariness before sinking back with his head in his hand. 'I'm sorry,' he repeated, 'I hardly knew what I was doing.'

'You might have been drowned.' Sara Shuddered, fresh in grief. 'My Father – Oh, you must know I'm *afraid* of the sea.'

'God, yes.' Chastened, Wickenham stood up, bedraggled, and sodden with water. 'Maybe we're all scared, deep down, and that's why it draws us. I was almost mesmerised out there.'

Sara was on the point of speech, wanting to ask him about the strange thing he had said on the sands, but she couldn't bring it to words. He looked at her questioningly, then stooped to pick up the basket. 'It may not work out so badly,' he said, trying to cheer her, 'if we must walk further upstream. Let's go. At least it will help to dry out my clothes.'

It was a drab anti-climax to the earlier contentment of the day, and the enforced trudge against time across unfamiliar terrain did nothing to lift their spirits. Already the shadows clawed at the remaining patches held by the setting sun and, above all, was the threat of inescapable retribution that faced them on their eventual return.

Keeping to the shoreline was not easy, for though rough tracks ran along the crest of the cliff, these often petered out among the thick brake or came to an abrupt stop on the edges of flooded creeks around which detours had to be made.

It was full grey dusk before the last of the inlets were cleared and they emerged on the flatter stretch of the river meadows. Here it was narrower, but the estuary was at its height – with the stream rippling against both banks. The sunset seemed to have drawn the breeze and almost all sounds down with it, leaving only faint murmurings in a trembling stillness.

In weary depression they moved to the brink and gazed anxiously over the water. There was still no sign of a bridge but, a little way up river, a patch of white glinted feebly in the fading light.

'It's a boat!' exclaimed Sara.

'It is,' Philip said, thankfully.

The little dinghy was tied to a crude landing stage set into the rock, straining at its rope like a living thing impatient to be on its way. No owner could be seen and no dwelling was visible. Wickenham hesitated only a second before drawing in the painter and helping Sara on board.

'We mustn't risk going on further,' he said, 'and surely our need is uppermost.'

The crossing was perilous, for Philip had scant boatmanship. The torrent swept the craft hopelessly upstream, and he could barely make out the opposite bank in the gloom. Sara crouched silent, fighting not only her dread of the water, but the sinuous fear of the night that enclosed them in that dismal place, where there was no sound but the rush of almost invisible water, and nothing to view but the twisted limbs of trees that beckoned like crones' fingers from the edge of the darkened field.

At last, exhausted, they made the safety of the bank and staggered ashore, drawing the boat up beyond the reach of the tide. Stumbling across the rough ground, they turned in the direction of Crigga where, far in the distance, a light flickered suddenly – then was lost to view.

'Bear up, Sara,' Philip encouraged, 'There must be a road. We shan't be long now …' He broke off. 'God in heaven, what's that?' As he spoke, there had been a fluttering of wings from somewhere behind them and a long, mournful shriek shattered the brooding peace. Again, and again it rose, a weird, blood-curdling wail – more like the cry of a stricken child than a bird. Then it faded mournfully away, leaving the estuary in haunted silence once more. 'My God, what was it?'

Sara clung to him, trembling, her face blanched, 'It's – it's a bird,' she faltered at length.

'A bird?' Wickenham echoed, 'What sort of bird makes a cry like that?'

'I don't know.' Her voice was low and awe-stricken. 'Some people say it's a warning – the crake – the lost soul of a man who did wrong and can't find peace. Oh, Philip, I can't stand this place.'

From the edge of some nearby trees, they saw the flash of a lantern, and a gruff voice was calling: 'Hello there! Sara! Where be 'ee? Sara! Sara …!'

CONTEST

In Crigga, another day with no sign of the fish had left the people moody and anxious. The season for the coming of the pilchards was passing, and seldom in memory had the shoals delayed their arrival for so long. Even the steadiest of the fisherfolk were beginning to look beyond natural causes for the root of their troubles, while the superstitious hotheads muttered constantly against the strangers, whose arrival had marked the beginning of bad fortune for them all.

In such an atmosphere, Luke Pemberthy and Joe Pendenna – dejected after their unrewarded vigil by the boats – came back to the cottage to find Elizabeth sitting by the fire alone, staring fixedly towards the open door. All day Luke had been uneasy at the thought of Sara's venturing to Pennan alone and one question only was in his mind. 'Where be the maid?' he asked.

The old woman transferred her gaze to him without answering, her eyes burning feverishly. 'Where *be* the maid?' she demanded again, reflecting her fire, 'Where *be* the maid, then? Where'm she to?'

Elizabeth kept her eyes on him. While the men had been watching for the fish, she had spent endless hours waiting and worrying in her own right. A sound rolled liquidly in her throat, a bitter chuckle, not far removed from the mindless cackle of a crone, 'Where be the maid, Luke?' she mocked. 'Where be the fish, then? Where be the good ways of Crigga? Where be the man from the grey house, then? Didn't I tell 'ee? Didn't I warn 'ee, so?'

Luke was a poor dealer in words. He motioned silence to Joe and crossed the kitchen to Elizabeth, gently placing his hands on her arm. 'There, do 'ee hush,' he comforted,

60

'What be 'ee saying? What about 'un, then, up at the grey house?'

Elizabeth began mumbling – more to herself than to Luke, 'She was with 'un this morning, out on the Pennan road with the third stranger. But where'm she to now? Didn't I tell 'ee? Tes the devil's work all over again.'

'Do 'ee hush, now.' The memories of a generation ago were as sour in his heart as Elizabeth's. His voice came hard and low, 'The good Lord shall keep the maid free from evil ways. Who told 'ee then, Mother? What be this about the Pennan road?'

Shaddy Bunt seen 'un,' she said, 'Go and find 'un, then, if 'ee can. Tes the devil's work, Luke, I did tell 'ee.'

'Do 'ee wait here, Mother.' He turned up the glimmer of lamplight, left the cottage and swung into action with Joe beside him.

Outside, a knot of neighbours was gathering, primed by their womenfolk on their return from the cliffside and quay. They respected Luke as one of the community's elders and rallied to him, partly in sympathy, partly welcoming the diversion from the disappointment about the shoals.

'Where be Shaddy?' Luke asked.

'Down to the inn,' someone said, but a young watcher demurred. 'He be up at the grey house again now, I seen 'un go.'

Luke nodded and started along Fore Street, the growing crowd with him. After a few steps he halted. The mutterings were becoming ugly, and tense though he was, violence was not natural to him. 'We'm too many,' he said, 'Just Joe and me will go to the grey house. The rest, look for the little maid.'

'Do 'ee take Polwyn, Toms, and Dan Bicknell on the road to the creeks,' ordered Joe, 'Tes likely she missed the tide.'

Greywalls loomed gaunt and mysterious in the starlight. No gleam showed from the front windows, and no sound came from inside.

The two men mounted the steps and Luke put a sinewy hand to the bell. The peals echoed and re-echoed with strange emptiness from the depths of the house. Soon there came a reflection of light through the glass-panelled door, as a lamp was turned up in the hall and the door opened. Clements appeared, peering first at them then past them into the gloom of the night.

'Why my dear soul,' she said, shaken at once from her taciturnity, 'What are 'ee after, then?'

'Nothing from a place good Cornish folk shouldn't be to,' Luke said, accusingly. 'Missus, where be that Shaddy Bunt?'

'What be that to you?'

'Luke's little maid be missing,' Joe told her, shortly, 'and Shaddy might know where she'm to.'

Clements looked at them primly, not without compassion. 'Wait then,' she said, 'and I'll tell 'un.'

In a few minutes he appeared in the doorway, pushing the last corner of pasty into his mouth and rubbing his hands. Luke eyed him contemptuously, but wasted no time.

'The maid still be away,' he said, 'What did 'ee see? Tell us proper now, Shaddy Bunt.'

Shadrach's revelation was little enough. He had seen Sara and the stranger walking away from Crigga along the Pennan path. ''Ent no business of mine,' he said.

'Tes business of all of us,' Luke told him, shortly, 'Leastwise, all who be true Crigga folk. Have 'ee seen 'un since – the furriner from this place?'

'He ent been back,' Shaddy said, ''Ent no call to get mazed with the likes o' me, Luke. *I* don't know where he'm to.'

Luke turned away, trying to smother the anger and shame in his soul. Two full days only had Sara been in their keeping, and now the whole village was witness to what she had done, fanning again the smouldering flame and re-opening the wounds her mother had left before her. He was only dimly aware of Pendenna's voice in his ear. 'I'll stand by 'ee,' Luke. Whatever befall, I'll be along by 'ee.'

They were nearly home when they noticed the crowd gathering in the road beyond the cottage. There were excited voices and a lantern flashed in the middle of the group. 'Scat 'un down,' someone was saying, 'let me get to 'un, I'll scat 'un across the chacks.' They reached the edge of the crowd unnoticed. At its centre stood the little band of searchers with Skipper Trebilcock in charge, closely surrounding Wickenham and Sara. It was as well Joe had picked sober men for the job and warned them against violence. Several of the fishermen would have attacked Wickenham on sight, and Trebilcock, large and tough as he was, found it hard to keep them at bay.

'Do 'ee hush!' Pendenna called loudly, 'Step aside now and let Luke look after his own.'

A sudden hush fell over the gathering. For a moment it was completely still, as though posing for a colourful tableau, as the men looked around. Then they parted to let Joe and Pemberthy through. Luke went slowly and deliberately towards Wickenham, who stood haggardly erect holding the basket, with a scared but defiant Sara holding onto his other arm.

'Tide cut 'un off,' said Trebilcock, breaking the silence.

'Did 'un then?' growled Joe.

At once, Sara pleaded for Wickenham. 'He helped me – honestly, he did, Grandfather. I'm sorry I'm late, but really, there's nothing wrong …'

Philip remained silent, bracing himself for whatever might come. Then, as the men waited, he spoke. 'It is true. I am sorry. But there is nothing more I can say.'

'Nothing, ezza?' challenged Joe, 'Then do 'ee answer to this …' Despite his appeal to the men he was inwardly seething, brooding still on the death and defection of Ruth, reading in Philip the hateful enmities present and past. The strain had mounted, threatened, and finally snapped his control. Pendenna broke. Before anyone could stop him, he lurched forward and pinned Wickenham by the throat. 'Take this for both of 'un, then and now!'

Sara screamed. Wickenham struggled, the basket spilled on the ground.

'I'll have 'un yet,' Joe glared at gasping Wickenham, 'I'll have the sod for the two of 'un. By Christ, it's more than a man can stand.'

'Leave 'un now,' Luke urged, quietly, 'Leave 'un, Joe. Do 'ee take the maid home.'

'Ess, I'll take the maid. Do 'ee hear?' Joe growled again at Wickenham. 'Leave Crigga to Crigga, mister. I'll take the maid.' He gathered the trembling Sara and led her through the now subdued crowd, then turned once more from its fringe. 'I'll have 'un,' he vowed, 'As Christ is my witness, I'll have 'un, you.'

'Amen,' muttered Luke. He crossed to Philip, and a raging shout would not have been more potent than the muted menace of his tone. 'Joe means 'un and so do we all if 'ee don't leave the maid be. Now how don't 'ee go, mister? How don't 'ee go to hell afore I do send 'ee there?'

Philip limped slowly away, not only with his throat ugly from scarlet wheals, but each strand of his sensitivity raw and inflamed – less from the threats of the fisherman than the barbs of his self-condemnation. He had throbbed with pain, but the greatest blow was to his ego. He had never been so crudely humiliated. To have been dragged from Sara like an erring child, publicly reviled as a philanderer, attacked with elemental violence, and warned off in front of a crowd … It was a sickening blow to his pride. He felt thoroughly disgraced and unclean.

Wickenham was no coward and, had the cause been worthier, he would have fought vigorously. But his conduct had been devious from the start. To pursue Sara now would not merely be damaging to himself, but create an even worse situation for her. He would have given much in those moments to have put the clock back to yesterday. Then he could have acted with reason and dignity. Now he had compromised Sara, been justly punished, and the only possible recompense was never to see her again. That the solution was so starkly uncomplicated was the most wounding realisation of all. Thoughts pounded relentlessly. He had agreed to help Sara. That promise could not be fulfilled.

Jeffries would know about this. If nothing else, Shaddy Bunt would relate the news. At the thought of his host's reactions – the anger at his careful advice being recklessly ignored – a fresh wave of despondency swept Wickenham. In his weary dejection, he was tempted to pack and leave Crigga at once but, even if this had been feasible at so late an hour, the slight to Jeffries would be unforgivable, the confrontation merely postponed.

Philip groaned. There was no retreat. Whatever the personal cost, he must face the issues and try to recover something of his self-esteem. Even with this resolve, he had to muster every shred of his courage to present himself on arrival back at the grey house. Luckily, Shaddy by now was thickly among the speculation that raged at the inn, and Clements gossiped with nobody. In her master's absence, she greeted the wretched guest with prudent neutrality, only arching her eyebrows at his dishevelled appearance and advising him that food was laid out in the dining room and that hot water was available if he needed a bath.

Eating was out of the question, but the bath was welcome and, when he was bathed and changed, he felt easier – though still morose. To stay indoors was impossible. Roaming the empty rooms aggravated his sense of loss. Asking Clements to leave one of the doors unlocked, he wandered again into the night.

On the breeze-ruffled crest of the headland, he found the rendezvous Sara had mentioned before – a bowl-shaped depression of turf above the harbour, overlooking the spray-washed cove. Far below the tumbling crests could be faintly seen, ghostlike as they wove eerie patterns in the rocks. Yet again, as he peered down, he experienced the perilous magnetism of wind and sea, and drew back from the edge to the inland side of the hollow.

Sara knew this place and, but for his impulsiveness, they might have sat here many times – and so differently. In the solitude of the summer darkness, with no-one to see or hear, Wickenham bowed his head in a crescendo of frustration and remorse. A phrase he had once heard burned into his consciousness: 'A soul makes its own Gehenna …' How true that was, and this hell was entirely of his own construction. 'God forgive me and help me to do right,' he murmured and, even as the plea came thick from his throat, he knew that if Hades itself beckoned, he would barter his soul for the touch of her hand.

The lamp burned for many hours in the Pemberthy cottage. Elizabeth would not be comforted. Though for years she had prophesied the third stranger's visitation, the actuality had jerked her back to the older memories, where she hovered by the threshold between mystical visioning and earthy wrath. Long ago she had banished Ruth. Now it took all Luke's persuasion to prevent her driving Sara the same way.

'Little bitch,' she muttered, 'tes Satan's work. Tes the first maid all over again. No good can come of 'un.'

'Hush, Mother, hush. Do 'ee blame the stranger, not the maid.'

'I do blame 'un both, and so will 'ee Luke, when the devil do strike …' And at last, from sheer weariness, she subsided into her secret world.

When the couple at last retired, a light still flickered in Sara's tiny room. Though chastened, and to a degree repentant, she could not bring herself to accept that the Crigga conventions were wholly right, or that her relationship with Wickenham must be automatically ended.

The chasm between the generations, always difficult to bridge, had been immeasurably stretched by the differences in outlook she had inherited as John Michal's daughter. She respected her grandparents' views, had dutifully bowed to their chiding, and would not willingly have hurt them, but the thought of surrendering unconditionally to their way of life, clashed head-on with her upbringing and very nature.

From the window she could pick out the lights of the grey house, and her thoughts were of the crowded events of the day and the new dimension so dramatically introduced into her life by the romantic stranger. She remembered the emotion charged walk, the dallying on the sands when she had unwittingly revealed her feelings to him, the explosive moment when they had so nearly kissed, the tortuous journey across the brake, the ghastly shrieking of the legendary crake.

Propped now on the truckle bed, the rush lamp writhing tormented shadows across the walls, she pensively thumbed through the one link with Wickenham none could deny her – the volume of verse. She had earlier recalled the darkly premonitory poem from which she had subconsciously quoted at the river's edge, and once more she began tracing its message from the dimly lit page. The phasing, the uncanny significance of the lines from Maelstrom fascinated and held her.

Helpless I ventured where the maelstroms lie,
And so must die,
Unless one pausing on the further shore
Turns and moves the small mountains,
Fashions the stepping stones
To draw me nigh.

Countless times, she read and re-read, attempting the deeper interpretations, trying to resist the temptation to personalise them: '... *Unless one pausing on the further shore/ turns, moves the small mountains* ...' A reference to faith overcoming all obstacles to love? And she loved him. Oh, she loved him from a depth that all the superficial tempests of convention were trying to destroy. Not just for the light he had shone on her exile, not because moved by the plaintive imagery of his verse, but with an instinctive elemental attraction that had punctuated evolution since time began. And like a flower blossoming in alien surroundings, the wonder of it was intensified by having germinated in such unpromising soil.

At last, as the rush lamp spluttered, she reluctantly laid down the book. Of Philip's own feelings she dared not guess, but had he not said, as he lay almost drowned by the swirling tide? '*The maelstrom – and you – you called me back from the shore* ...'

TENSIONS

After a relentless night, Wickenham spent the next morning licking his wounds in retreat by the derelict harbour – scene of his ill-chosen rendezvous with Sara. None came to watch for the pilchards, and in the peaceful surroundings he sought to restore some of his shaken dignity. The bruises to his pride were hidden, but those on his neck showed vividly. Jeffries was due to return in the evening, and the thought of having to face him in such a state was shattering.

Towards lunchtime he wandered back to the house in time to glimpse Shaddy shuffling furtively away from the outer door of the conservatory. The little man glanced shiftily around, hesitated, looked guiltily towards the conservatory, and came unsteadily across.

'Still up-along then, mister? So, Joe ent come after 'ee, yet?'

Philip inwardly cringed. The last thing he wanted was goading from Shadrach. 'Mind your own business, Bunt,' he said shortly, 'You're a damn sly fellow. Get on with your work.'

'Sly, ezza? Who went off with the maid?' Shaddy gloated, studying the marks on Wickenham's throat. 'Ent no call to fret about *me*. Just keep clear o' they Crigga maids. Joe'll see to 'ee else.'

Normally surly, Shadrach had never dared to speak so openly as this. Now, with the master away and his breath potent with alcohol, he found the courage. 'If Joe don't, there's plenty who will. And if they don't, then Crigga will. What say to that then, mister?'

Philip said nothing. He was tempted to a scathing retort but desisted. His ego was battered enough, without being whittled still further by crude verbal exchanges. He continued towards the conservatory.

'Don't 'ee go in there now,' Shaddy called after him, 'Ent nothing for 'ee in there.'

Set-faced, Philip went in. The place looked much the same, though he noticed the padlock securing the trapdoor now had a key in it. The air was odorous, and on the table stood the evidence of a half empty bottle. The atmosphere was alien, but no apparition appeared. Sickened, he passed through to the inner room.

'Get 'ee gone.' Shaddy's mumble came from the doorway, 'Ghosties'll have 'un, else.'

With a cursory glance at Shaddy, Phillip went.

Jeffries stormed in just before dinner. He sought Philip out in the library, took one outraged look at the wheals on his neck and tackled him without benefit of finesse.

'So, it's true. Goddamn my soul, it's true. Are you out of your mind, boy? God's blood, didn't I warn you enough?'

Till then, Jeffries' wrath had only been sensed. Now Philip shook to the actuality. Sick with chagrin, he stood his ground, wishing for the hundredth time he had been more circumspect. 'I'm sorry,' he managed to say.

'Sorry? Sorry, bedamned, you're a grown man, not a boy caught scrumping apples. I want an explanation, sir, and a good one.'

'I just carried a girl's basket to Pennan.'

'Just carried her basket? Dear God, is that all you can say? Didn't you think about me? Greywalls? Your own good name? Damn it, sir, I thought you had sense and responsibility.'

'So did I. It was crazy. But it was only one stupid mistake.'

'One? *Once*? Damn you, isn't that more than enough? I've had Shaddy Bunt smirking, fists shaken in my face all along the road,' growled the outraged Jeffries, 'Your damn *once* has set me back years, and we'll be lucky if it ends there.' Fiery of face, he began pacing the room, then stopped at a side table and reached for a bottle, 'God's souls, I need this. And so will you. What about Catherine – your wife, sir? That's even more damnable. Had you no loyalty to her?'

Stung, Philip accepted the drink. 'You know me better than that. Let's keep a sense of proportion. Anywhere but Crigga, this would have been nothing.'

'But this *is* Crigga.'

'Yes, and only here would it have been wrong – boy scrumping apples or not,' Philip said. 'I'm truly sorry. I've been a fool, but it will never happen again.'

Jeffries grunted, re-filling his glass and mellowing slightly as the alcohol circulated his frame. 'What's done is done, I suppose, and I'll have to live with it.' He lowered himself into his favourite chair. 'Alright, alright. I've always known you a man of principle, Wickenham. Didn't bring you all this way to quarrel and cuss, eh? Not over some slip of a gal who means nothing to you.'

'I didn't say that.'

'Eh?' Jeffries bristled again, 'By God, you'd better.'

Wickenham, tense, gave look for look, 'Sara is an exceptional person, but I've told you, I shall not see her again.'

'By God, I should say not. Of all the damned dangerous ground …'

'You knew her parents, I think …' Philip began, but Jeffries stopped him.

'Enough. Bought one of the chap's paintings, that's all. Now forget it – her, him and the whole damn business. They were on the road to hell, Wickenham. No concern, whatever, of ours.'

Philip risked one more attempt. 'How do you mean?'

Jeffries, erupting, pointed towards the door. 'I've said

enough, damn you. Do *you* go, or do *I* go? Or do we stay and talk about civilised matters?'

The reaction seemed absurdly out of proportion with the enquiry. Even at the first, Jeffries had not been so incensed. As a guest, as a protégé, as a tactician, Philip could do nothing but concede – though inwardly he was wide with wondering. He inclined his head. 'I'm sorry. Of course, there's no need for either of us to go.'

Gradually Jeffries calmed down. 'Of course, of course. Had a deucedly long day. Didn't expect all this. Sit down, Philip. Never want to hear of these people again – not the parents, never the gal. It's over.'

'And the civilised matters?' Philip was too tight-lipped for temper's hackles to rub off.

There was a space while Jeffries replenished the glasses. Then, predictably: 'Your work, Catherine,' he said.

'She wrote to you, didn't she?' Philip was perversely glad that some of the heat lingered. In the flush of argument, it was easier to talk. In cold blood, this would have been intolerable.

Jeffries eyed him directly. 'Yes, she wrote to me. No blame to her, Philip. She's worried about your attitude, your work, your marriage. Thought I might have a word with you, eh? Asked my advice.'

'So?' Philip was pan-faced. This time it was a mundane snare weaving in on him, the lasso that must draw him back to what the world knew as normality.

'A poor tool, advice – to give or to use,' Jeffries admitted. 'I feel damnably useless. But I care for you both. Can't help noticing things, eh? Only wish you were happier.'

'What is, *is*,' Wickenham said, 'We married in haste and are basically different. Our ways don't tally. We must just learn to live with it.'

'Something is missing,' Jeffries said, bluntly, 'and not only that, your work is suffering.' He held up his hand, 'Alright, you're not entirely to blame, but let it be said. Your first volume was good. Doing well, glad to have it on the list. But where is the second? We need it to establish you. Where is it?'

'I'm doing my best.'

'No doubt you are, but it won't materialise – not the way we want it – till the other thing is resolved.'

'The other thing?'

'Your marriage for both of your sakes – contentment, stability ...'

'Not inspiration, by any chance? Not the freedom to soar?' Philip was bitter.

'Poppycock,' grunted Jeffries, 'If you have inner contentment you can soar to the stars from a London cellar as poetically as from a moonlit garden.' He shook his head. 'Alright, damned if I want to lecture, but I did promise Catherine ... Is it too late, Philip, eh? Impossible for both of you to move a bit nearer the centre, try to pick up the threads and do something with them?'

'The old threads, you mean? The ones that have already been picked up, used, and found wanting?'

'Alright. Find a new thread, then, make something worthwhile with that?'

Philip looked at his host and smiled wanly. 'Of course, I want to make Catherine happier if I can, but we've run out of possibilities.' He was determined to be honest.

Jeffries sighed and pushed back his chair. He was fast running out of avuncular solutions. 'Dinner will be on the way. We'd best get along. Think on this, Philip. Think on it eh?' He placed a hand on Wickenham's shoulder. 'She loves you, Philip, and you're still young enough.' He tapped Philip earnestly. 'Is it possible, perhaps, that a child might make a difference? Eh? For both of you?'

73

Wickenham shrank from his touch. 'A *child*? Is that what you want? An innocent pot of glue to stick us together?'

'No, damn it,' said Jeffries, 'I'm serious. I want her happiness. Think of *Catherine*, Philip. Always think of *her*, my boy.'

HEVVA!

As more days dragged by with no sign of the pilchards, the resentment of the frustrated fishermen steadily mounted. Shaddy became an obvious target for abuse when he went on his rounds, and at night disgruntled watchers began to congregate outside Greywalls chanting, 'Go back to where 'ee came from. Go back!' Once, sticks and stones rattled into the garden and against the lower windows and door.

After that, Jeffries ordered the shutters to be closed on the ground floor and, as the tension grew, forbade Wickenham to venture too far outside. 'They've the double grudge against you,' he warned, staring angrily across the placid bay, 'Why the hell don't the fish come and be done with it?'

In deference to his host's wishes, Wickenham accepted the confinement to Greywalls philosophically, though his heart was still heavy and he longed for the solace of open spaces. Meanwhile, the presence of Jeffries and the increasing excitement at least helped to take his mind from the renunciation of Sara.

The windows of the grey house became a grandstand from which to view the spectacle on the cliffs, the prologue unfolding before the main characters entered and high drama began. From the upper floors, the cast appeared strung along the headland like marionettes waiting to be motivated by the puppeteer familiar of the fish. But still there was no enactment. Still the surface of the bay remained tantalisingly unbroken by the shoals, and angry murmur rumbled out across the bay and the granite of Greywalls.

Soon after lunch, Wickenham could stand no more of the incarceration and suspense. Leaving Jeffries dozing sonorously in a library armchair, he crept quietly through the wall door in the kitchen garden and made his way slowly to the old harbour. Here, he could relax for a while, and still be on hand to witness the netting of the shoals if the fish should come.

But more was contained in Philip's fate than the destiny of the shoals. As irrevocably as a pebble drops into the water and sends ripples dimpling to the shore, the vibrations set up by his arrival in Crigga had enmeshed him by the chain of events he had put in motion. Carefully, though he had crossed from Greywalls from the site of the ruined quay, a watcher had seen him and followed. He had stood only a minute, gazing on the tumbling breakers, when the crunch of hurrying footsteps came from the shingle behind him. He knew, instinctively, before he had fully swung round, that there was no escape - knew the pain and bitter ecstasy of foreordination. Yet still, like a fly impaled on a pin, struggled vainly and hopelessly to break free.

'Philip,' Sara called softly, and the emotions he had fought for days to stifle began to surface and take life once more. She stood against the background of cliff, hair tumbling back from the sea gusts, a half pleading, half enquiring expression in her eyes. She was dressed simply and plainly for work in the cellars, her trustfulness and absence of guile touching him deeply. Yet he knew, for everybody's sake, he must not be moved.

'Oh, Sara, you should not have come.' Despite an attempt at gentle chiding, the words emerged more as a gesture than a reproof.

'But I did. I had to.' She was quick to respond to the underlying warmth of his tone. 'I saw you and followed you.'

'That was unwise. You might have been seen.'

'I am not quite a prisoner,' she said, with a quick toss

of the head. 'Philip – don't be unkind to me, please. After the other night, I just had to see you again.'

'Yes, it was a poor sort of ending.'

'Then *why*?' she entreated.

'Because it *was* the ending. And you already know why.' Unable to meet the directness of her gaze, Wickenham turned back towards the waves. He sensed, rather than felt, her movement beside him.

'Every night I've been up to my place on the headland,' she told him, 'I hoped you would come.'

'I was there the very first evening, after the Pennan walk,' he answered. 'After that …' His hand almost closed on her fingers, but he resisted, his whole substance at war with itself. 'Oh Sara, you must understand. Already this has brought nothing but unhappiness to everyone.'

'Not completely. Not to everyone.' She said nothing more for a while, watching pensively, with Wickenham, the rollers creaming into the desolate harbour and the sun glinting into the curtain of spray. Then, with quiet persistence, 'Whatever it means, I must see you, if only once more. There is no-one else I can talk to, and so much that I want to say.'

'And that you must *not* say.' For a moment he relaxed, turning and with a controlled wonder, allowing himself to cup her head in his hands and smooth the hair from her temples. 'You must go, Sara. They may be looking for you, and there will be more trouble if you are seen with me.'

'Trouble there be!'

Philip swung quickly to face Pendenna, who had kept Sara in his sight as she made for the other side of the headland. He had come up silently, till his voice and the crunch of his feet on the shingle had made them turn.

'Trouble there be.' Pendenna knew nothing of subtlety

or finesse. His tone was a jagged blade severing the link between them. 'Trouble enough, maid, for the stranger – and 'ee – if 'ee don't go back along.'

Wickenham let his arms drop to the side, exasperated that his honest intentions should have foundered in such a miserable way, and strongly conscious of the futility of argument. Sara was more positive, swivelling to face Pendenna with a flash of the sudden independence Philip had grown to admire. 'There was no need to spy on me, Joe.'

Pendenna halted, gazing grimly from one to the other. 'Tes for the good of 'ee. Now let me deal with the stranger and get 'ee back to the quay – afore Luke do find where you'm to.'

'You'd better go, Sara,' urged Philip.

Pendenna turned on him swiftly. 'I did warn 'ee to go, mister. And when she does, by Christ I'll teach 'ee once and for all to stop seeking after this Crigga maid.'

'I'm not a Crigga maid, and leave him alone,' Sara flashed, 'I came here alone. He didn't know I was coming.'

'Didn't he so? Then he do be making the best of 'un now.'

Pendenna's mouth was set harshly – his eyes, truculent slits, focusing his concern for Sara and all the recent frustrations of Crigga. Wickenham, too, was seething, forgetful even of his promise to Jeffries, itching to get to grips with the man whose very presence symbolised the hopelessness of his feelings for Sara.

'Get 'ee along, maid …' Pendenna laid a firm hand on her arm.

The attitude of mastery and Sara's spirited tug of resistance, finally thrust Wickenham to boiling point. 'Leave her alone,' he commanded.

'*What* do 'ee say?' Joe swung again, savagely eager.

'I said leave her alone. Let her go by herself.' Philip was rigid with passion. 'Take your hands off her, Pendenna.'

Slowly and positively, the fisherman put Sara aside and, ignoring her protests, the men faced each other on the lonely beach like gladiators in an empty amphitheatre, only the gulls screaming in witness.

'Fight then,' Pendenna ordered, 'By Jesus, I'll show 'ee. Ent no Luke Pemberthy to save 'ee now.'

He inched forward, his arm swinging back to strike, but the second he did so, as though his action was a conductor's sign to a hidden orchestra, a sound rose sudden and clear above the turmoil of the surf and the overtures of conflict; a sound all Crigga had waited and prayed for and almost given up hope of hearing after the weary days of suspense; a sound so unmistakable, so distinctive, that Pendenna froze like a statue with his fist up-swung and stood listening – his expression a wry mingling of deprivation, thankfulness and disbelief.

Again, the sound came, the high mellow note of a horn, vibrating across the headland and to all recesses of the clustered dwellings and, with the first hum of voices, murmuring upwards and outwards like the drone of distant bees from a disturbed hive. The cries crystallized and soared to a crescendo.

'Hevva! Hevva!' And once more the horn sounded, 'Hevva! The fish be coming! Tes the fish, the fish!' Sara echoed, 'Joe, Joe! It's the fish, the fish!' The relief in her voice was partly for Crigga, partly for the seemingly miraculous answer to a personal prayer. 'Hurry!' she urged, 'Joe! The cry is up!'

Pendenna needed no prompting. The instinctive fisherman in him responded to the trumpet call like a warrior to battle. For only a second, he stared back at Wickenham, his eyes blank with the vision of another world. Then he flung up his head and added his shout to the din swelling up from the further cliffs – where now people could be seen dancing and running.

'Hevva! Hevva! Jesus be praised, tes the fish at last. Hurry, hurry maid! Hurry!'

Wickenham watched them go in a tumult of feeling. Joe Pendenna was running, now heedless of everything but his dedication to the fish. Sara went more slowly, torn between a reluctance to leave and her duty to the Crigga folk. Just once she turned, their glances meeting for a moment in an unspoken pledge. Then she wheeled and followed Pendenna out of sight over the headland hump.

THE COMING OF THE FISH

Infected by the swelling excitement, Wickenham began making his way to the opposite cliffs, pausing only when, from the edge of his eye, he noticed a familiar figure coming from the direction of Greywalls.

'Thank God,' the bluff Jeffries said, 'now perhaps we shall get some peace.' He looked quizzically at Philip. 'Damn it, man, you must have been out here already.'

Wickenham nodded, briefly. 'Down by the old harbour. Where are you heading?'

Jeffries was puffing a little. He waved an arm towards the Huer's Hut without committing himself to speech, and they hurried on. There was no point now in attempting concealment. With the sighting of the shoals, strangers and feuds were temporarily forgotten. There was too much work to be done.

'Hevva! Hevva!' By now the cry was being taken up by a thousand throats, a wild psalm of triumph and thankfulness that was relayed along the waiting coastline and over hill and field, till it reached inshore hamlets whose people rarely ventured towards the sea. In Pennan the ancient bells rang, and a baptism came to a sudden end as one and all ran from the church. Carts were wheeled out, horses saddled, and the long trek to Crigga began. In Crigga itself every chore stopped, every pint in the inn was abandoned, every able man and woman went running. From church and chapel, Sunday school teachers came tumbling together. All was apparent confusion – people hurrying and shouting, scrambling down cliff paths to cellars, beaches, and quayside, launching boats not already afloat, cussing, laughing, and incessantly repeating the joyful chorus: 'Hevva! Hevva!' For the pilchards had come at last. Up on the headland crest, infected by the universal excitement, Jeffries and Wickenham joined the small group still looking out across the bay.

'There,' Jeffries pointed, 'and there.'

Completely new to the sight, Philip at first found difficulty in distinguishing any difference from the normal appearance of the bay, mottled and glinting with ruffles of spray and reflected lights. Then, as he focused his eyes more closely, came the gradual realisation. Today, the colourings – not merely of unusual tinting – were flecked with silvery reddish brown among the blue-greens and the white. Where these new patterns shimmered in great patches across the water, they were almost solidly organic – vast stretches of the bay were literally alive with fish, so densely shoaled that they were leaping and jostling each other from the water as they moved along.

'Hundreds of 'em,' muttered Jeffries, as the glittering masses moved slowly nearer and drifted parallel to the shore, 'literally hundreds, eh? No wonder Crigga thinks they're worth waiting for.'

But it was not enough that the fish had arrived in the shallows. Swift action was necessary if they were to be secured before they turned and headed for the deeps again. Wickenham watched in fascination as work began on the encirclement of the shoals. First, rowing cleanly across the inshore waters, the leader of the seine boats – Luke Pemberthy, Joe Pendenna, Skipper Trebilcock, Tom Biddick, and the like – each to an allotted segment of bay, each with several tons of carefully stowed seine net aboard, and each with an expectant eye on the huers who, from their vantage point, directed each one with a megaphone, and signals waved from white cloth tied on a stick. Little by little the shoals were surrounded and divided, the encircling boats dropping the weighted nets until the pilchards were contained by a barrier of mesh and channelled towards the shore. In this way, a series of enclosures was created along the beaches, each full of many hundreds of thousands of trapped fish. From apparent chaos emerged a system of well drilled activity. Once the seines were drawn inshore and the ends made fast to each other, the first vital stage was over, but the long stints of harvesting and packing remained. For these purposes every possible source of help was called upon, the labour graded according to age, experience, and ability – from the leading fisherman who kept close watch on the tides, weather, and safety of the seines, to the unskilled who did the fetching and carrying from beaches to cellars and the routine chores.

'Go and see for yourself, eh?' Jeffries suggested. Perhaps I can go and catch up on my interrupted snooze.'

On the beaches, carts were already arriving and being organised into orderly columns to haul the catch. In charge of one of them stood Shaddy, in complete abandonment of Greywalls and all that it stood for. He glared with distaste at Wickenham and turned his eyes back to the harvesting of the fish.

Philip recognised, from what Jeffries had told him, the smaller nets, or 'tuck-seines' attached within the main seines. These secondary nets had long ropes attached which, when hauled upon, drew some of the enclosed catch to the surface, to be scooped up in baskets and emptied into the boats. Men were working feverishly at this, piling the pilchards up high, sculling the loads to the shore, tipping them into baskets, barrels, and carts, and returning quickly for more. As each receptacle and vehicle was filled the woman or man in charge moved off, straining up towards the honeycomb of cellars set into the lower cliffs. Everybody was happy in the first flush of effort, singing and shouting, 'Hevva! Hevva!' and entirely ignoring the watching stranger. Laughter and talk also drifted down from the cellars, where women had begun bulking and salting the fish.

On the approach of evening, Wickenham left the bustle of the beaches and followed the carts up there. The cellars were gloomy, lanterns flickering in their dusky interiors, casting strange shadows on the toiling women. At the entrance to the rough-hewn caverns, barrows and carts ceaselessly deposited their loads for women and children to build neatly against the rear walls. As each layer was completed, salt was sprinkled thickly upon it and the next level began. Not an able soul in Crigga seemed to be without a task, and the din from people and horses, marauding gulls, and creaking wagons, could be heard over a great distance. The labour went on far into the night, almost through to the following dawn, till the last of the catch was cleared from the seines and safely salted down in the cellars.

All was not undiluted labour. At times, after hours of steady work, the toilers stopped for a while and congregated on the upper flats to rest and consume pasties and ale, and discuss overall progress. Whenever these breaks occurred, Philip tactfully withdrew and went – either to Greywalls for his own refreshment, or simply roamed the temporarily deserted beaches and cliffs.

Philip strayed beyond the quay walls. Crigga, that night, was a haven of absolute calm. The air was still, the bay lay at ease with barely a ripple marking the ebbing tide. A half-moon scooped the horizon like an overblown sponge absorbing the emotional spillages of the day – the harbour lights, liquid reflections of green across the wet sand. He paused for a space, then cautiously picked his way around the rocks along the edge of the sea. The tide was far out and the soft lap of the moon-glinting water delighted him. He was heading now, with uncaring awareness, towards the notorious cove – treacherous in the annuls of Crigga lore where even experienced fisherfolk had been cornered and drowned. But the night drew him onwards and he had no fears. He rounded the sharp spur of rock past which – when the tide turned to flood there was no return – then trod into a great sandy cavern within whose lofty arches smugglers of old had cached their contraband. He stepped further in, warily groping into growing darkness, then stood listening to the regular drip-drop of water into the pools of the cave. Suddenly he tensed, sensing a stealthy movement behind him.

'Philip, take care …'

From the disharmonies of the last days, it was as though the whole headland had broken into song. She could not see him against the monotone of the rock face, but he could dimly make out her silhouette as she paused in the half moonlight filtering through the narrow entrance. Her presence there seemed natural, as though this eerie place had been waiting for them to meet. Ghostly, extra-dimensional, bizarre, this was his true world – whatever the strictures of mundane existence might demand.

'I knew you would come here,' he heard her say.

'They will miss you.'

'No. Not for a while. Come to me, Philip.'

Too choked to answer, he watched in wonder as her outline moved and was dissolved in the shadows of the cave. He came forward, guiding her by the sound, and instinctively she found him and sank into his arms.

'I love you, Philip, I love you …'

There were no other greetings, no regrets for the discarded bonds of convention. They clung together in the twilight of the cave and the sound of the soft, murmuring tide for a boundless age, lips and tears mingling in wordless rapture.

Afterwards they lay close, Sara tracing his nearness with tender hands and whispering half articulate expressions of love. Philip, content, held her in intimate silence.

Reluctantly, Sara broke the spell. 'We must go, my love. This is a most dangerous place.'

He roused slowly, his only answer a protective squeeze of her arm.

'You are quiet.'

Taking her head in his hands, he kissed her.

She sensed, without seeing, his smile.

'There is always sadness in rare happiness. Knowing that it can never happen again.'

'But it can. It must.'

'Never quite the same.'

'Then it will be new happiness. Oh, Philip,' she said, earnestly, 'you know it was *meant* to be.'

He continued to hold her, not trusting himself to speak. What was meant to be had been. It had unfolded naturally – without deceit. The real sadness was not that it could not happen again but that it must not, for only a planned deception could make it possible.

'We *must* go,' Sara was saying, 'We shall be caught by the tide.'

'Then we shall die together.' He intended it lightly, but the words echoed ominously in the dank surround, and Sara shuddered.

'No, please don't mock. There have been many tragedies here. An hour or most on a calm tide, they warned me, then the trap closes again. Come, we must hurry, my love.' She indicated the spur of jagged rock as they went back, pointing out a great boulder at its base. 'When that is dry, the tide is safely at full ebb. If wet, it is death to linger for long.' To emphasise her warning, ripples were already splashing their shoes.

'Yet you followed me,' he said.

'I know now, I would follow you even to death.'

'Oh, Sara,' he said, moved, 'I do not deserve your love – or your trust.'

She smiled faintly as they picked their way to safety over the last of the fringing rocks. 'Can we help what we feel, what we do? There, now we're safe. But there's the other danger, you know. We dare not be seen.'

'Then goodbye.'

'No, my dear love, not goodbye. I will see you soon. I *must*.' She looked around quickly, put up her lips to be kissed and, with a last contented sigh, left him.

He watched with a strange pride and hopeless longing as she trod warily towards the harbour path: 'Sadness in rare happiness ...' The truth in the words engulfed him. The very joy of the chance meeting strengthened his resolve not to see her again. His promise to Jeffries made it impossible. He dared not linger in Crigga or he would be completely lost.

She turned once and cautiously waved, and he raised a hand in response then, with a last glance at the scene of their idyll, slowly followed her back.

From the mists of enchantment, neither had noticed a third shuffling of footprints marked in the sand, or looked up to glimpse the figure of Shaddy Bunt slyly retreat from the brink of the lower cliff.

CAVERNS

The activities were over – almost as quickly as they had begun. Wickenham went down on the second morning to find that the last seine had been emptied, the nets were being retrieved, most of the cellars had been closed, and only a few stragglers stood around on the quay. The main body of workers had dispersed to their homes for a well-won sleep. Further demands would later be made of them, for the pilchards would have to be barrelled and transported for export abroad and sold to the villages around. The remainder would be conserved for home consumption, and the oil pressed from the catch salvaged for lighting purposes.

Meanwhile, the great thing was that the fish had come, been sighted, netted, and salted down, to bring substance once more to the old Cornish jingle: *Meat, money, and light, all in one night...* And later would come the celebration in thanksgiving for the harvest of the sea.

Completion of the pilchard harvesting heralded an emotional anti-climax, with nothing for Wickenham now but a dead scene underlining his moribund hopes. On returning to Greywalls, he went to the drawing room where he brooded by the window – to savour the aftermath. His mood was for solitude, an uninhabited seclusion where he could wander or sit and mull over patterns that might have been. Resolution is little defence against romance, and he longed with a torturing intensity for a chance to see Sara just once again. He hoped where there was no hope, flayed himself with the whips of impossible fantasy. Her image was never far from his mind. Now it persisted until, dreamlike, it was framed in his consciousness as an inviting picture. Inevitably, he thought of the John Michal canvas, and soon, without surprise, found himself being drawn to the north wing.

The lure was still there in the ante-room – the old painting depicting the sweep of a virgin headland, with the fisher-girl gazing plaintively over the dappled bay. Fascinated, he studied the features, so like the living Sara in line and expression. It was as though she was striving to speak to him. Then, as before, reality blurred and he succumbed to a shimmering magnetism gently impelling him through the conservatory door.

Inside it appeared much the same, but today there was one difference: the heavy trapdoor was unlocked and lay fully back on its hinges. And it was from there that the coaxing emanation was strongest. Intrigued, Philip crossed and glanced into the opening. Nothing much could be seen from that angle, but a short ladder was fixed to the side. Without hesitation, he cautiously descended.

It was a small low-roofed chamber, which at first seemed a normal cellar, but was, in fact, an inspection pit serving to check on the foundations of the house – which at this point appeared to be built across a pitted surface. Great masses of cement supported reinforcing girders, forming a solid bridge. On the headland side, opposite the foundations proper, the ground had also been strengthened, though less impenetrably. Baulks of timber bastioned small, irregular cavities, from one of which a narrow tunnel ran down below the rock. The headland, so apparently firm above, was evidently to some extent honeycombed in this way.

As his eyes became used to the dim light, a secondary use of the pit became evident – in the cache of bottles Shaddy Bunt had contrived to transfer from his master's own cellar, and from which he had obviously been celebrating the coming of the fish in his own way.

Philip hardly noticed this, too vividly aware of the

strong force now engulfing him. The gentler persuasion remained, but the dankly oppressive atmosphere had introduced a new element, with darker, more sinister overtones that sent a chill through him. The emphasis here was of doom, of voices crying in helpless pleading, and a sensed rumble like distant thunder.

All outside the confines of his mind was as silent as a tomb – a tomb bolted and barrelled against the intrusion of the years. Philip was as stable as anyone, but the insistence of inner tumult terrified and unnerved him till he could bear it no longer. Suddenly he wanted to run, to get far away from this haunting chasm. He took a step backward, turned and made for the sanctuary of the trapdoor, just as it clattered down to engulf him in utter darkness. For a moment he stood petrified. Then, in near panic, struck savagely at the door.

'Let me out! For God's sake, whoever you are, let me out!' For a space the entire cellar seemed vibrant with mocking laughter. There was no movement, no sound from above. He called again, urgently, 'Open there! Open up! You've shut me in!'

And then a thick, guttural voice echoed, chuckling and taunting. 'Eh? How do 'ee like that then, mister? Gone after they ghosties, have 'ee?'

'Damn you, open this door!'

'Open 'un? Darn 'ee, I've got 'ee like a crab in a pot.' An obscene laugh floated down through the planking. 'Be 'ee after they Crigga maids, dead or alive? *She* be down there, mister. Joe did send her down there – now I've sent *'ee* …' A gloating chuckle again, 'Three of them there was, but two got away. You ent getting away, mister. How did 'ee think that? Stay where 'ee be, with the maid …' The voice went on, slurring with drink and vindictiveness. 'I told 'ee I'd get 'ee.'

'Let me out, damn you. *Shaddy Bunt!*'

'Bunt! Damn your eyes, what's all this?' To Philip's enormous relief it was Jeffries' gruff interruption. 'Move, damn you, man. Open that door.'

The ring of outraged authority penetrated even Shaddy's befuddled state. A thin gleam of light welcomed Philip, the trapdoor creaked fully open and he thankfully emerged to Jeffries' wondering stare. Shaddy lounged by the table, eyes glazed and an uncomprehending grin on his face.

'Bunt,' Jeffries demanded, 'what the hell's going on down here?'

Shaddy waved a nerveless hand and sought an excuse. 'Cleanin',' he mumbled. 'Cleanin' un out, you.'

'Cleaning, be damned. You're drunk.' Jeffries swept a hand towards the bottles, outraged, 'And on my very best brandy. You'll pay for it, Bunt, and by God you'll be lucky if I don't give you the sack.'

'Sack, ezza?' Shaddy Bunt roused, steadied with difficulty, and aimed an accusing finger at Philip. 'This be your doin, enna? Getting' all mazed – down-along with the maid. I'll get 'ee next time, mister. I'll see 'ee don't bother they Crigga maids …'

'Get out!' Jeffries barked, furiously, 'By God, I'll deal with you later.'

'Ess, and I'll deal with 'un, proper. I'll shut 'un in for good.' Mumbling thickly at Philip, Shadrach lurched to the door.

When he had gone, Jeffries turned to Philip, standing in disarray, face flushed, jacket and hair smothered in cobwebs.

'For God's sake what *is* all this, eh, Philip? Eh?'

'Saw the trap-door open, had a look in, then he closed it. It was horrible.'

Jeffries looked at him keenly. 'Take care. That man isn't always responsible for his actions. And he has a special dislike for you.'

'What did he mean? Joe and the maid? And Joe sent her there? What maid?'

'Man's a fool,' Jeffries growled, 'Damn drunken fool. Take no heed of that nonsense.'

'No,' Philip persisted, 'there's more to it than that. It was strange down there, too strange for my liking.'

Jeffries eyed him for a while in exasperation. At last: 'Alright, alright. Damn his eyes, I've done all I can to forget. The Pemberthy girl was killed. Night of the riot. No fault of mine. Eh?'

'And Joe?'

Jeffries hesitated. 'Look, Philip, clean up and come up to the library. We can't talk here.'

Over drinks, Philip heard for the first time the full story of Ruth and John Michal – and Jeffries' part in the aftermath. Now he understood all the tensions, the fears, the suspicions, the misunderstandings, and overflowed with a newer compassion for Sara.

'It's over, and now let's forget the whole wretched business,' Jeffries concluded.

'I think Sara should know.'

'Sara should *not* know.' Jeffries was adamant. '*What* should she know? That her grandfather and the rest of them hounded her mother to death? That they were her virtual murderers? Don't let your emotions blind you, Philip. What good would it do, eh? The gal would be worse off than she is now. Let sleeping dogs lie, let these people sort out things in their own way, in their own time. It's no business of yours or mine.'

'But it's tied up with Greywalls,' Philip objected.

'I don't want it tied up with Greywalls. I want it *forgotten*. There's talk already of spells and disaster and retribution. Oh, yes ...' he grimaced at Philip's surprise, 'I've heard – damn them all. *You* know how the rascal

Bunt chatters in his cups.'

'And you believe all that?'

'My boy,' Jeffries said, seriously, 'it's the fool who doesn't believe. The wise keep an open mind.' He clipped a cigar, lit it, savoured the first fragrant puffs, 'No, I neither believe – nor disbelieve like a fool. But Crigga's a strange place, and there may be some who are gifted at glimpsing the lights that cast shadows before. Curses have been laid on Greywalls and the ways of its strangers. Ruth Pemberthy died miserably. John Michal suffered a lot. Few things have ever gone right for this house. Coincidence, eh? But I've learned not to tempt the gods – or the devil.' He rose, crossed to the window, looked earnestly at Philip. 'Consider – through Greywalls my life can be strongly affected. Through mine, yours - through both of us, Catherine's. Let it rest, Philip. Superstition or no, let Crigga go its own way, and we go ours. Otherwise, we're on the road to more and more trouble.' He paused, then continued reluctantly. 'The cellar? Yes, damn it, I've felt that too. It's a grave, and somewhere down there, far below, are the bones of Ruth Pemberthy. I try to keep clear, not to think of it. And that's my advice to you.'

As Philip strolled before lunch while the publisher carried on working, he brooded under a renewed fit of depression. Jeffries was right. To seek Sara, tell her what he knew of the truth, then leave her alone to face the reality, was unthinkable. He could only hope that somehow, in Crigga custom, the whole tangle could be resolved, that somewhere she would eventually find solace and happiness. In the same moments he knew – with a stab of pain – in such a hope, he was utterly deceiving himself.

Rousing from reverie, he found that he had wandered aimlessly along the middle cliff path he had taken on his very first visit. There stood the Pemberthy cottage, jutting from the rock like a square boulder of the cliff itself. Below the uneven plateau lay the cavern of poignant memory, haunted not only by the spirits of men who had been trapped by the tide, but the girl he had loved there and vowed never to see again. He peered over the edge, drawn irresistibly towards the sea, viewing the cave and surrounds as a single feature for the first time. Now, with the tide low and the sun lambent, the cove seemed safe enough. It was formed by an inlet surmounted by a series of perpendicular crags, up which, as evident from the markings, the tidal waters swirled high. The deceptively placid swell held the power of a cobra, which could release its tensions in a pitiless strike, transforming the inlet into an inescapable trap.

Philip's eyes scaled higher, where the cliff soared dizzily, pitted with smaller caverns, and revealing a perilous overhang at its crest. This must be the very place he had looked down upon the night he returned from Pennan. Somewhere up there would be Sara's secret haven. With a futile nostalgia he retraced his steps back past the cottage, up the zig-zag patch where he had found the volume of poems, and higher again until he reached the Huer's Hut, now entirely deserted – its annual function performed. A lark rose suddenly, throating its lyrical decibels against the cacophony of gulls. If seagulls really do contain the lost souls of men, Philip mused, the Creator could hardly have found a better haven for gulls. Their dismal wailing added to his own despondency. He moved dejectedly towards the hut. Then at last, he turned to the sheltered hollow on the cliff's edge.

Without intention, but with psychic certainty, he knew what he must discover. She lay back among the headland grasses, her eyes closed, perfectly relaxed. It was like coming home, to pause on a threshold where he had a natural right to be, but had steeled himself against entering. The key had been offered him, but in fairness must be thrown away.

His first impulse was to go forward. His second, prompted by conscience, to retreat and leave her without speaking. Then it was too late. Sara stirred and, in the same moment, opened her eyes.

'I knew you would come,' she said.

Philip smiled wanly. He went down the ridge and sank to the ground beside her.

'I must be honest. I didn't intend to come.'

'But you came.' She dismissed his confession, gazing up at him happily. 'Isn't it lovely up here? I could stay forever.'

'Won't they miss you at home?'

'Home?' Her face wrinkled, wistfully. 'My father used to say that a house was only emptiness with bricks around it – until the right people could share it.' She smiled suddenly again. 'It's me – it's my fault. I'm just not the right person for a house. I belong out here.'

'But when summer goes?'

'People make their own summers and winters. You should know that.'

He returned her smile. 'A stairway to Paradise or a road to Gehenna.'

'The road doesn't matter, as long as we can be together. And you belong here too. I feel it – this is *our* place – this and …' Her voice faltered. 'This and the wonderful cave …' The cave could mean only one thing to them now. She lowered her eyes. 'Philip – you don't regret what happened?'

'Only that it cannot happen again.'

Her brow wrinkled, and for a moment she was subdued. Then: 'It could if we had faith. We *must* have faith, mustn't we?'

'We must do what is right, Sara.'

'What is right for each other,' she quickly insisted. 'Oh, Philip, *why* are you so *afraid*? Don't you see we were *meant* for each other?'

Wickenham was silent.

'If we were,' she went on, 'there is nothing in the world we can do about it.'

'There is,' he said sadly, 'We must consider others and what we can honourably do.'

The words came out twisted and she was quick to sense the pain in them. She put out a hand impulsively to touch him, shivering when he drew coldly away. 'You mean Catherine?'

'I mean Catherine and Crigga and your grandparents. And all the trouble I have already caused.'

'Yet you loved me. You would have fought for me.'

'I would have done what I thought was right.' He dared not look fully at her or in any way risk committing himself, yet this time he did not resist the pressure of her hand.

'You keep saying that. What *is* right?' she demanded, 'For me to be miserable here? For you *and* Catherine to be unhappy in London? For everyone to go on making everyone else unhappy? *That* isn't right.'

He nodded, distressed. *She* was right. What was eternally wrong was the old drab, shabby, ineffectual triangle. He could find no easy reply.

'*We* are right, Philip dear,' she persisted, 'Nothing can alter that. It is too beautiful not to be true. I knew from the very first day at Pennan. Even before that. I would never, never agree to our parting.'

'Oh, my dear love. If only it was as simple as that.'

'But it *is*.' There was the glint of a tear on her cheeks – but the sign of truth in her eyes. 'It is simple and beautiful and lovely. The complications are not us. They are other people.'

'But they matter. We can't build happiness on the unhappiness of others.'

'But they were words – set pieces – not to be pitted against emotion and flesh and blood.' Sara would have none of them. 'When I first came to Crigga,' she said quietly, 'a few weeks after father had died, I wanted to die. I didn't want to be a fisher-girl. Everything had gone. I didn't know which way to turn. Then I met you – in Crigga, of all places. I met you and I became alive again. Oh, my love, do you think now, I could ever let you go?'

The sun went in for a while, and though the fringe of cliff sheltered them, they could see the eddying of breeze ruffling the topmost grasses like the cold touch of a wraith from the sea. The shade of John Michal, perhaps, who had wooed Sara's mother on this headland – maybe at this very spot. The shadow passed and Sara urged softly, 'Philip – you remember the maelstrom? We can find a way to move the small mountains. If we try …'

She was very close to him, her lips gently brushing his hand, and he could feel her breath wafting in warm whispers across his fingers. At that moment he almost broke, fighting a deep, secret battle with self he could barely recognise. He longed to take her in his arms, let the passion of the cave and the generations' history repeat itself, sweeping all moral barriers down. With a great effort he managed to say, 'The mountains must never be moved, my love, not in a dishonourable cause.'

She was about to plead again. Then she looked up and saw his profile, taut with inner conflict and despair, and her own great longing melted in the warmth of compassion for him. 'Please don't be sad,' she consoled, 'We can still meet here and discuss your poetry, and all the things we love – can't we?' Still Wickenham stared into the distance with the set, strained look on his face.

'Can't we? she prompted anxiously, 'There is no-one else, anywhere, that I can even talk to.'

He nodded vaguely and stood up, gazing beyond her to that other dimension in which there was no sea, no cliff, no briefly-glimpsed dream, but only the tyranny of street and office and social round.

'*Can't* we?' Sara asked for the third time.

'Alright.' He was barely audible. He felt for and pressed her hand briefly, still without looking at her. 'Alright. I must go now – but I will see you again very soon.'

With the lie burning his throat, he turned miserably away. It was not until then that he realised he was now also a hypocrite, that in his smug martyrdom he had condemned her to lost hope. He would have turned back, but could not face her. Worse, torn and divided by circumstance – he could not face himself.

Most of Crigga lay sleeping, but with the catch safely harvested it had reverted to the normal patterns of birth, life, and death. Once in the street, in tune with his own bleakness, a funeral procession assembled, the coffin draped on a handcart flanked by mourners, while the stillness resounded to the dismal clang of a minute bell: '*I heard a church bell ring ...*' The phrase droned at him from the Purgatory of his mind ... '*Heard it? No, knew it rang ...*'

Chanting dully, he repeated the lines, then extended it in embryonic verse –   '*I heard a church bell ring ... Heard it? No, knew it rang –*

Just as the sea beat murmuringly
And I heard it not, and the curlew scream
Wavered to me unsung,
And each unbelieving eye ...'

He could hardly see. Dear God, which world *was* he in? The universe of cold realities, where sea boots stomped the cobbles and decaying flesh was borne in a ritual box? Or this elusive haven of poetry, beauty, idealism, where in visioning he could walk with Sara, and know with her what he sensed to be All-Life? Or this intermediate Gehenna of futile suspension, of unbreathed passion and unspoken, torturing farewell?

He looked back and dimly saw Sara standing on the lip of her secret height, watching him till the instant he must disappear and, in his intention, out of her life forever. He raised an arm slowly in token, and the insistent Muse beat once more on his consciousness, intoning the finale till it was scored ineradicably on his mind –

'So, moments sped. Moments, but aeons died.
There in my stricken world I trod eternities
On deathless shores, mocked by the ceaseless
Tide of memories,
And ever each echo lied.
Whence came such strange unease?
Wherefrom such coma strayed – and why?
How need you ask me? You who have known
goodbye?'

He returned in late afternoon, the poem complete, his mind racked by resolution. Jeffries was still in his beloved library pouring over masterpieces already born and dreaming of lusty volumes yet to be sired. He looked sharply at Wickenham's face, white, strained, tight-lipped.

'Philip,' he said with concern, 'What the devil's the matter, boy?' Then with sudden perception, 'My God, man. After all we've said – you've been seeing that gal again.'

'By accident only,' Philip explained flatly, 'It's finished. Tomorrow I'm returning to London.'

'Wise,' Jeffries nodded, 'Don't want to lose you of course, but wise, very wise – In the circumstances, eh? Let it all blow over. Get back to Catherine, get on with the work. Then come again. Always a place for you, Philip. Always a place, my boy …'Tactfully, he asked no more questions.

Shaddy Bunt did – unrepentant, on the drive to the station next morning, his nose forever sniffing the ground for dramatic odours. 'Goin' back to that there Lunnon, are 'ee? How be that, then? Getting away from Pendenna, ezza?'

He drew nothing from Wickenham, who sat silently in the jingle, his back to the inshore cottages and his eyes fixed rigidly on the bay.

The water was effervescing with spray. Foam rustled like liquid lace along the foot of the cliffs and, when the corner was turned to the station, he could clearly trace the cove – with its overhanging sanctuary above.

Even now Sara might be there, waiting trustfully for his promised return. His heart went out to her. And it was in that moment that he became finally aware of the hopeless division within himself. Here, his physical frame trudged through the motions, willed to continue its appointed ways. But within was another, unfettered self, destined to answer from timelessness whenever the voice of Sara Michal should call.

INTRUSION

Sara, mending nets on the quay, had not seen the jingle take Philip to the station. When, from the leering Bunt, she heard that her lover had gone, the news struck like a physical blow.

'Best stay where 'ee be,' Shaddy Bunt gloated, 'Else we'll see 'un off proper – me, and Joe, you.'

Sickened, Sara turned without answering and made for the furthest point of the headland, to gaze without seeing into the seething mass of reefs below. That Philip should have left in such a way after all they had been to each other, without a goodbye, an explanation, or even the most cryptic of messages, was beyond belief. After the first shock she refused to credit it and it was only after two desolate days of waiting, searching, and watching by the grey house in all their remembered haunts, that she at last bowed to reality.

'Oh God,' she prayed on the second night, gazing with blurred eyes from the headland hollow to the dark pile of Greywalls, 'Why? Why did you bring him to me only to take him away? Please, please bring him back …' It was as though all Crigga mocked her in reply – from the brooding rocks in the bleak wind, and from the distant estuary, the distant cry of the crake.

Days and weeks went by without any word or sign of Philip, yet still Sara held to a diminishing hope, wandering the cliffs in a mist of loneliness and haunting – whenever she could – the station road. Seclusion she could endure, and the bitter solace of her own melancholy.

Much harder to bear were the whisperings and attitudes of the villagers, Elizabeth's of accusing awareness, the Crigga folk critically aloof. Her affinity with the stranger had been sensed if not seen. Even without that, she could never have been a true Crigga maid, and now Philip had gone she felt the full impact of difference and isolation.

Only Shaddy was vocal, blatantly waspish whenever he passed her alone. 'Ent come back for 'un, maid, and lucky for 'un, or they'll have 'un proper…'

But of all Crigga, Joe, in an obstinate, dog-like way, was becoming the greatest problem, clumsily trying to make amends. Unavoidably, they were thrown together in working hours, and he often approached her at the Pemberthy cottage at night, awkwardly seeking friendliness – till even the balm of escape to solitude was threatened. Opportunities for retreat became rarer, her stresses increasingly intense. And still she held desperately to the hope that one day Philip would keep his promise and come back.

One evening, loth to return to the Pemberthy hearth, she went straight from the quay to the clifftop hollow. She was particularly sad that night. Silence seemed to throb in the now autumn dusk, stars vied with the rising moon, and the whole scene was pregnant with memories of Philip, his words, his verses: *Again, the jewelled nightcap of the stars, / And the grey gown of dusk …*

'Philip, Philip,' she murmured into the grasses, 'Why did you leave me? Please, please come back …'

There were footsteps, and the twilight deepened where a shadow fell. Startled, she turned.

'Maid,' said a voice, 'Maid, what be 'ee doing here?'

'Joe!' To Sara it was as though he had desecrated holy ground. Uncomprehending, Pendenna stepped forward.

'Joe! Leave me alone.'

'No. Tes time we did talk,' Pendenna said.

'Somewhere else, Joe. Some other time.'

'No,' he insisted, 'this be as good a place as any. You

be getting mazed, all this a-wandering and brooding. Luke do be worried, maid.'

'Then let him speak.'

'No,' Joe said for the third time, 'Luke don't rightly know what to say. But I do want to speak to 'ee, Sara – proper and true.'

Dismayed, she remained silent. Haltingly, with gruff kindliness, Pendenna went on. 'Pining ent going to bring 'un back.'

'Who?' She was agitated, off guard.

'You do know who, maid. The stranger, a wed man, a furriner. Best mind that and forget 'un. Best be a Crigga maid.'

'But I'm *not*!' At last, she found response, stirred by the mention of Philip. 'I'm not, and you can never make me.'

'Ess I will, the good Lord willing.' Joe sat beside her, simple, incongruous in the setting, wholly unable to plumb the true depth of her feelings – yet sincere. Time had mellowed him in all respects except his implacable opposition to the strangers, whom he blamed utterly for the death of Ruth. Secretly, he had mourned for his own part in it, for his own lost maid – whose image in Sara was before him now. 'You and God willing,' he said with rough honesty, 'I'll take 'ee and look after 'ee proper.' He hesitated. 'What do 'ee say then, maid?'

Sara froze. 'What on earth do you mean, Joe?'

'You know what I do mean. I would wed 'ee, maid. What do 'ee say?'

Sara said nothing. Her throat was dry, unresponsive. She had never actively disliked Joe, but the thought of marriage to him was petrifying, obscene.

Misreading her silence, Joe spoke again, 'Ess, I would wed 'ee, maid. But not till I tell 'un the truth. I'll not speak for 'ee without telling 'ee, maid.'

'Telling me what?' Sara managed to falter. She wanted to cry, to scream, to run from this waking nightmare, yet knew she could not escape.

'I'll tell 'ee, maid, God forgive me. I'll tell 'ee...' Suddenly, the guilt damned up in his mind and overflowed. In his own way, truly but without finesse, he told her the story of the rioting at the grey house, the chase, and its tragic ending. ''Tes only right you do know. I would have wed the mother, and I would wed the child – but not until 'ee do know ...'

Sara listened, shivering, repelled, as the grim secret unfolded. The revelation could not have been more appallingly timed. In different circumstances, with Philip to turn to in sympathy and understanding, she might have absorbed and related it. In these surroundings, on top of all her desolation and despair, the realisation was horrific. She wanted to run, yet knowing that whatever she did the horror would remain with her.

Joe spoke again, anxiously. 'I do be sorry, maid, right sorry for 'un, that be the truth. But I had to tell 'ee afore we got wed.'

'*Wed*?' Sara's voice was almost inaudible, but the misery rang through.

'Ess. Now 'ee do know all, but I be speaking for 'ee. I'll look after 'ee, maid, be a father to 'ee – naught else.'

'A father?' The thought of Joe taking the place of beloved John Michal stung Sara at last. She rose to her feet, facing him, concentrating words into one bitter statement of repulsion. 'You wanted to marry my mother? You killed her? And now you would marry *me*?' Her lips narrowed in a tense whisper. '*I'd sooner die.*'

'Maid, *maid* ...' His painful effort in ruins, Joe made a final appeal. ''Tes all in the past. I did say I was sorry. I'll look after 'ee, true ...' Then, as she still stared at him aghast, slow anger began reddening his cheeks. ''Tes the stranger, enna? Wed an' all, enna? He be cheatin' 'ee, maid, like the one afore 'un did to your mother. And him up to the grey house. Tes them brought death and vexation to Crigga, maid, not the likes o' we.' In momentary passion he reached out, grasping her shoulders. 'I tell 'ee, you'll wed me, maid. Ent nothing else for 'ee now.'

'Don't touch me! Don't *speak* to me!' In her distress, Sara wrenched herself clear and ran – down the slope, past the grey house and the old harbour, and into the chill obscurity of the dunes – where, the weeping of the mind, somehow withheld through the barren weeks, burst in a flood of tears. 'Dear God,' she sobbed, 'what am I to do?' And in response to her plea, the answer came from her lips: 'Philip, my Philip!'

In her pride, despite all the heartache, she had vowed never to make the first approach – for his sake – but to continue in Crigga was now quite impossible, and there was no-one else in the world to whom she could turn. When she was calmer, she went cautiously back to the cottage – fearful of being pursued by Joe. But Pendenna had retreated to ponder his next move, his animosity to the stranger intensified. Her grandparents greeted her resignedly – Luke with a glance of silent concern, Elizabeth with the usual strange murmurings and accusatory nods.

Sara lay awake for many hours that night, racked by the evening's events and a yet unnameable fear born from the one cherished idyll with Philip. At last, sure that her grandparents were asleep, she silently crouched by the flickering rushlight and, with preciously hoarded paper and pencil, began to write.

Days later, the letter arrived in a routine batch from Jeffries' publishing house. It could not have come at a more fateful moment – when Philip's forlorn attempt to retrieve his marriage had reached breaking point. During the weeks of separation, the turmoil in his mind had matched Sara's own. The grand gesture of renunciation had solved nothing and benefited nobody. His work had suffered, Jeffries was more censorious, Catherine increasingly distrustful but, most of all, he was haunted by his desertion of Sara. What had seemed right at the time now appeared grievously wrong – leaving her as it did, with false hope and a shallow lie. He longed to make amends, but like Sara, pride, and the fear of making matters even worse held him back. Instead, he strove to justify the betrayal by honouring his obligations to Catherine, and this proved even more disastrous. Catherine, already highly critical, had noticed the change in him on his return from Crigga, sensed a feminine influence and, without directly challenging him, made her discontent obvious. Though unspoken, her doubts put an even more wounding edge to their already brittle relationship, and from mutual frustration bitter quarrels were born.

This morning there had been a particularly hurtful exchange, culminating in her tearful departure for consolation to the ever-indulgent Jeffries, a ploy she was increasingly using as a weapon against Wickenham.

For Philip, the entire situation was becoming intolerable. The strain showed on his face, his bearing, and the miserable quality and quantity of the work he had to force himself to produce. Today, as he sat disconsolately at his study desk, the effort was quite beyond him. He lowered his head on his arms, yearning with all his being for some escape. 'How long?' he muttered, fervently, 'How long, oh, Lord, how long?'

Wearily he roused himself, toying absently with the still unopened mail, as if therein lay the reply. It was a small collection: an account or two, a charitable appeal, a couple of appreciations – or otherwise – from readers of his verse. He shuffled them listlessly, with complete indifference, then tensed.

The envelope was plain, flimsy, lying obscurely towards the bottom of the pile, but to Philip it gleamed like a homing fire. It was addressed in pencil, in a neat hand, and bore the Crigga postmark. He withdrew it carefully, and it was as though a light had entered the room, as if fingers had reached out from the century of headland and sea to comfort and reassure his own. 'Sara!'

Overcome, holding the unopened letter, he crossed to the window. He saw nothing, for an inner mist seemed to be shrouding his eyes. He waited until it passed then, with trembling hands, opened the envelope.

'*My dear, dear Philip, do forgive me for writing. I did not intend to, but there is nowhere else I can turn...Oh, why have you left me like this?... It is awful... They want me to marry Joe...*'

'Dear God!' Philip murmured. Despite his conscience-stricken imaginings, he saw clearly for the first time just what he had condemned her to: the futile waiting, the fears, the loneliness, the communal solution of a loveless wedlock. He shuddered and continued to read.

'*But there is more: I fear, I greatly fear ...*'

For a moment he lifted his eyes, unwilling to accept the words into his senses.

'*I greatly fear that I may be pregnant. Please, please, Philip, what am I to do?*'

Slowly he crushed the pages in his hand, gazing before him, and this time the mist in his eyes was real. Action was called for now. For a long while he stood, battling with his emotions, then placed the letter on the fire and left the house – walking and thinking till late afternoon. When he returned, he made his decision. Catherine was still absent. He closed himself in his study and, tense with new resolve, penned his reply.

'*Please forgive me. I thought it better for all concerned not to see you again or even write, but now I know I was wrong. Do not worry. At whatever cost I will come to you – very, very soon. It would be unwise to reveal my plan in a letter, but I will be in Crigga, God willing, two days after writing this. Watch carefully for my arrival, and meet me either on the cliff or in the cave – whichever the tide allows. The cave would be safer...*'

He ended with encouraging words and, after some moments of hesitation, sealed and posted the letter.

TREACHERY

The commitment was made, and Philip concentrated all his energies into putting the plan into operation. It was not easy. Not deceitful by nature, he spent the next day in a torment of tension – fearful that a look or a careless word would betray his intentions. Thankfully, Catherine was in the depressed aftermath of yesterday's upheaval and showed little desire to communicate. To his relief, she left the house in mid-morning, leaving him in in solitude. Painfully he composed a letter to her, regretting that their life together had now proved impossible and that he was leaving, never to return, but that he would ensure proper provision would be made for her. Then he too went out, to draw a substantial sum from the bank, and to arrange at the nearest cab rank for a conveyance to be available at midnight.

On his return, he packed a sturdy bag with the most vital of his documents and manuscripts and, when Catherine was safely retired, he propped his farewell note on the breakfast room table and, like a thief, crept cautiously from the house. The cab was waiting to carry him to the station where, a fugitive from all that his past striving had stood for, he sheltered in the waiting room until the following day.

Sleepless and needled with guilt, monstrous fears harried his mind. He felt every finger pointing at him, shrank with every swing of the door, half expecting Jeffries, Catherine or – in his bemused state – even Pendenna – suddenly to emerge and challenge him.

At last, with a great surge of thankfulness, he was safely on his way – the train howling a symbolic screech of farewell as it groaned from the station. The journey seemed interminable, intensifying the strains that had been building up through two anxious days but, by mid-evening on a drear wintry day, he stood once more on the platform of Crigga station. He had travelled unobtrusively, and still lingered in the background as the few passengers dispersed. When the station had emptied, he made for the exit barrier and strolled diffidently through the almost deserted yard, where he stood for a moment scanning into the darkness.

'What 'ee be doin' down-along then, mister?'

The tone was gruff and unfriendly. Too late, he swung to see Shaddy Bunt, pausing with beady-eyed curiosity from his task of hauling parcels into the jingle. Philip cursed himself for his carelessness. Of all people in Crigga, Shadrach was the last person he wanted to see, and the most likely for him to have come across – especially on the London train.

'What be this, then? Nobody said nothing.' Shaddy finished his loading and challenged him. 'Clements ent expectin' 'ee, that I do know.'

Philip wanted to answer back, but checked the frustration in time. Whatever the cost to his nerves he must try to remain cool. 'Clements will know soon enough.' He forced himself to restrain his exasperation. 'There was no time to write.'

Bunt still stood akimbo. 'Where be the master, Jeffries, then?'

'He isn't here yet.' Shaddy's eyes seemed to screw into him. 'He's coming later.' There was an element of truth in that.

'Furriners. Darn Lunnon furriners. Never know where they'm to.' Shaddy spat. Then jerking a thumb at the jingle, 'Best get 'ee in, then.'

Again, Philip agonised. To go through the charade of arriving at Greywalls, telling more lies, then to abscond with Sara, was unthinkable. Clements was the one other person he could not possibly face. Yet to refuse the lift was against all normal practice. Damn Shaddy Bunt who, from his very first moments in Crigga, had dogged his affairs. Only the thought of trusting Sara, and the promise that this time he dared not break, prevented him from turning and running from the man.

'Darn 'ee. get 'ee in the jingle, will 'ee?' Shaddy grumbled, 'I ent got all night, mister.' He indicated the small space left among the strewn parcels, prompting Philip's excuse.

'There's too little room in there. I'll walk – stretch my legs after the journey.' He spoke with renewed authority. 'Since you're in a hurry, you can get along to the house.'

'Do 'ee get walking, then,' Shaddy looked at him cunningly, 'Ent no concern o' mine.' Disgruntled he made to move off, but on an impulse, Philip stopped him.

'By the way …' He spoke carelessly, 'How is the tide tonight?'

Shaddy glanced at him curiously. 'The tide, ezza?'

'Yes. Is it coming or going?'

Shadrach hesitated, fiddling with his whip, staring at Philp, then turning his eyes shiftily away. 'Tide be out, mister, far out and ebbing,' he said at last and, with a flick of the reins, urged the jingle out of sight, leaving Philip contemplating the empty yard.

It was a sombre stroll through the lowering dark, the way crowded with memories. There were no watchers on the cliffs tonight, none peopled the road but the wraiths of imagination. Philip walked stealthily on, glad to be alone with his thoughts and fears. His plan had been to go with Sara through the night to Teffry – the first railway station up the line – and to discuss this arrangement at their preliminary meeting. Now there was the complication of Clements who would be expecting him at Greywalls, concerned when he failed to appear. It was vital to get to Sara quickly – before the alarm was raised.

Philip was rigid with tension as the grey silhouette of the Pemberthy cottage came into view. A lamp glowed by its kitchen window and, as he drew near, keeping well into the shadows, there came a stab of light from the upstairs casement. It flickered and held, and when he came abreast a shadow loomed at the curtain, and the fabric was drawn. With caught breath he trod slowly past, raising a hand in brief acknowledgement. Then assured that Sara had noticed him, he walked cautiously towards the harbour path.

The quayside was greenly lit by the rays of the guiding lamp. Little could be seen, though the distant murmur of breakers proclaimed the sea's normal restlessness. For anyone to seek the cove on that night was madness. Wickenham, befogged by weariness and the strain of events and, with memories of their last perfect idyll flooding his mind, took the uneven path, confident that Sara would be following him again. Barely able to see in the blackness beyond the harbour, he picked his way gingerly along the base of the rocks and, as his eyes adjusted to the gloom, he could just see the boulder Sara had shown him as a safe guide to the state of the tide. It was uncovered. He stumbled on further, and eventually groped his way past the jutting spur and turned into the mouth of the cave.

Up on the headland road, at the foot of the track which led to the grey house, Shaddy halted the jingle and peered uncertainly into the night. After a while he got down, tied the pony's reins to a marking post and began walking towards the cliff.

'Ho there, what be 'ee after, Bunt?' The stocky figure of Pendenna materialised from the gloom, his facial lines knitted into a web of suspicion. 'What be doing then, Shadrach?'

'Tes the stranger from Lunnon.'

'And what of 'un? Where be?'

Shaddy Bunt hesitated before pronouncing the momentous words. 'Down to the cove.'

'Cove, ezza?' Pendenna said grimly. 'How do 'ee know that?'

'He did say.'

Pendenna scowled. 'He did say? How didn't 'ee stop 'un, then? You do know well enough the tide be turning to flood. Darn 'ee, Bunt, we'd best go and stop 'un, now.'

Sheepishly, Shaddy began following Joe. Suddenly, Pendenna halted.

'Do 'ee hush, Shadrach,' he warned, 'There goes the maid.'

A slight patch of white moved to their right through the darkness, on its way to the higher cliff.

'He ent down to the cove,' Pendenna breathed, harshly, 'and as well for 'ee, too.' He pointed to the headland crest, '*That's* where he do be. I'll scat 'un this time, then. I'll stop 'un for good.'

'Ess, and I'll come along with 'ee. Darn furriner,' Shaddy muttered, vindictively, 'I'll teach 'un, you. I did say I'd get even with 'un, Joe …' Submerged in a wave of victorious excitement, he deserted the jingle and crept stealthily behind the fisherman as Sara disappeared into the darkness.

In the Stygian depths of the cavern – isolated with his thoughts – Wickenham waited, wondering why Sara had not yet come. He was sure she had been at the window and seen him go past, certain that with the tide at full ebb she would have recognised the cave as the safest place to meet. He began to fear she had fallen or lost her way in the dark. 'Sara!' He heard himself calling, 'Saaraa! Saaraa! I'm here!' The cries echoed hollowly from the confines of the rock, weird discords that seemed to hang forever in that desolate place, but no answer came. Suddenly, with a long thrill of horror, he became conscious of the swirl of icy water running over his shoes.

Even before he had fumbled in panic to the dimly outlined entrance, he knew he was trapped, that the maelstrom was claiming its own at last. The tide, in full rampant flood, was funnelling into the narrow opening of the cove, and for any hope at all he would have to force a way round it. He lunged forward, but in a second the waves were buffeting his waist, lifting him off his feet. It was not so much the depth but the backward suction that rendered him powerless, first dashing him inwards, then raising him and flinging him helpless into the curling menace of the following wave. He struggled desperately, but the unending conflict of waters gripped and held him, would not let him go. Mentally and physically the agony was mercilessly prolonged: the horror of belated realisation, the relentless pounding, the soaking and dragging down of heavy clothing. Desperately, he tore off first greatcoat then jacket, but it was all too inadequate, too late. A freezing tower of ocean engulfed him, then another. Bruised and numbed, he made one final, despairing effort to battle round the cruel spur of rock, but the currents cupped him with liquid fingers and tossed him contemptuously back.

Somehow, he got hold of a ledge slippery with seaweed and surging water. Then from the rising sea loomed the forerunner of a mounting series of waves. The first struck him and hurled him pebble-wise against the jags of rock. The second threw him higher as he frantically strove to maintain a precarious handhold on the ledge. Engulfed and weakened in tide-race, the handhold became a fingerhold clawing futilely at the pitiless face of the cliff. And then came the monstrous crest of the third wave, swelling tall and threatening above him.

In the fear of impending destruction, his very soul cried out. It was the voice of conscience, now, of elemental regret transcending physical pain and registering with psychic impulse on the cliff and cave, 'Oh, God!' he shrieked, a second before a great comber wrenched him from the rock, 'Sara! Saraa!'

The cry rose in strangling pipe to merge with her answering scream from the cliff-top, to be snatched into mocking orchestration by the wind, 'Philip! Philip!'

'Sara! Saraa!'

The desolate discord guided Shadrach and Joe as they hurried towards the crest, where she hung, clinging on the very lip of the precipice. Once more the cry soared, in eldritch unison, then the voice from below was abruptly silenced. She would have plunged in futile sacrifice downwards, but Pendenna reached out in time and drew her shivering from the brink.

'Dear Christ, forgive us all for this night,' he muttered. 'There, I've got 'ee safe, little maid. Now do 'ee let Crigga look after its own.'

Unbelieving, unseeing, Sara lifted her eyes to him, her grief-stricken pleading almost inaudible. He bent his head down to catch the words.

'Philip,' she cried, 'Oh, *Philip*...'

And a sudden hush fell upon the headland.

RETURN FROM GEHENNA

But Wickenham did not die. The killer wave had fallen short of its task. It was as though Poseidon, in a rare act of mercy, had scooped him up on the end of his trident and tossed him safely ashore.

In a further act of mercy, glancing upwards beyond the cliff, a wagon rolled along a narrow track. It proclaimed: Soames' Mission. The evangelist reined in his horse where the track grew widest, fixed its nosebag, and prepared to brew tea. But first he took the air, shuddering at the chill in it, and glanced aslant the bay. The tide was way out, and the sun glinted feebly down on the shore in the cold of the early morning. Suddenly, Soames squinted, for he was certain he saw a man slumped on the shingle, arms outstretched as though clutching at nothing. 'Yes, indeed,' he murmured, and began groping his way down the steep, rough-hewn steps to a beach strewn with seaweed and flotsam. 'Hello, there!' he called, 'Help is on its way.'

The prostrated man did not stir, and the saviour evangelist, gathered pace to reach the unfortunate soul. He moved closer and checked for a pulse, but at first nothing throbbed. Then he discerned the faintest trace – a thread, intermittent, barely there. 'God be praised. Sir, sir, are you alright, sir?' Still there was no reply. 'Oh, my dear Lord! Stay there. Don't you move.'

Soames quickly retraced his way back to the wagon to fetch a small bottle of brandy, and returning, pressed it insistently against the man's lips. 'Now sir, let some of that course through your veins, and let me help you to the wagon.' Slowly and deliberately, they made their way.

In the warmth of the van, Soames dug out from a dishevelled pile, an old fisherman's jersey, and an over-large pair of trousers. Assisting him he joked, 'Oh, now, it seems, I'm turning you into a scarecrow!' His brow immediately crumpled. 'But I am remiss. It is no time for levity.' Wickenham said nothing, but weakly smiled as a token of thanks. Soames handed him a mug of tea and a sandwich of potted pilchard – a welcome repast. 'Now,' he continued, 'I have done one good deed for the day – but I see there may be more to come.' A rarity of pure goodness, Soames continued in concern for the battered soul before him, 'My dear young man, you must tell me all about it all and how I can be of assistance to you …'

But Philip, after days of anguish and a fight with the rampant ocean, entered the arms of Morpheus, curled under a blanket and slept. And still he slept … He awoke, some hours later to clopping of hooves and the rattle of sundry pots in the back of the wagon. Startled, he pulled the canvas flap back at the rear, to reveal a high-hedged country road winding behind him. The driver of the vehicle was in full throat singing a hymn, heedless of Wickenham calling out to him. Wickenham called louder: 'Stop!'

'Whoa…!' Eventually, turning by a stream with a lush helping of grazing, the wagon wheels squeaked to a clumsy stop. Soames unharnessed the horse and joined Philip, who was sitting perplexed on a heap in the wagon. 'Ah, so you're awake at last. It's good to see you recovered.'

'Where the devil am I?' Philip asked, anxiously.

'Somewhere near Dawlish, I imagine,' the evangelist replied.

'Dawlish? So far from home?'

'I was unable to wake you,' Soames explained, 'and you were in a terrible way. Caught by the tide, I would imagine, and by the grace of God, lucky to get away with it. It's a miracle. That's what it is, a miracle. Oh, they do

117

happen, you know, they do happen.'

'I must thank you for my life. But Dawlish, when I should be …? He stroked his brow, feeling vague, anxious to recollect. 'Oh, God, where should I be?'

'I'm afraid I can't help you. I was hoping you could recover earlier so that I could put you on a train in the right direction, but looking like this …'

'It would be ludicrous.' For the first time Philip softened, and laughed, feebly, and thought it strange how humour had the ability to intrude when one least expected it.

'And anyway,' continued Soames, 'you're still suffering from shock, from a mild concussion, I suspect. I had to keep you in my care. I didn't want them to put you in an institution – or even gaol – but had to get back to London.' He reached up to a shelf and brought down a stout leather bag. 'Would this be of any help at all?'

Philip turned it over, slow to recognise it, then raised his brow. 'This is mine, I think. How did you come by it?'

'Again, by the grace of God. It was washed up with you on the shore. It's good, strong leather. It should be alright inside.'

The small key was missing but, with the right implement made available to him, Philip prised the lock open, at once revealing important manuscripts, documents, a change of linen and a large amount of money. He looked puzzled. 'I was well prepared, but where was I going – and what on earth was I doing in the sea?'

'You did mention getting to the halt at Teffry.'

'I have no idea what that means, or …' Then it struck him. 'It was the next station out of …' Elusive thoughts goaded him.

'Crigga. That's where I found you – in the bay.'

Soames busied himself with the refreshment. 'You couldn't remember your name.'

'Philip, Philip Wickenham,' he revealed, thumbing through his papers, and extracting his book of verse.

'The poet?'

'If you wish to call me that, I suppose I am,' he answered vaguely.

'I do and I will. I have your book of verse, and very edifying it is too. Let me introduce myself – Soames – an evangelist – and a great admirer of your work. Surely – no, it's not possible, and I am actually in your presence?' He indulged in a lengthy handshake, before extracting a book of verse from a muddle of boxes and tracing the titles with his finger. '*Maelstrom*, that's the one – *move the small mountains ...*'

It was then that the image of Sara came to him, and little by little the whole sorry saga began to unfold in Wickenham's recovering mind, and the reason for his ill-fated rendezvous with Sara. He had left his wife, and her last words, which had then rung discordant, now made him recoil.

'Poetry – what's that? Why can't you have a proper profession, instead of shutting yourself away day after day, trying to soar ...? You realise that Uncle Jeffries who made you can break you, don't you?' She had thrown back her head in cynical laughter, encouraging him to step forward to strike her. 'Go on, I dare you to do it!' But he dropped his raised arm to his side and she left the house.

It was soon after that that he had read Sara's letter, in which she had appealed to him, and he knew then that there had been only one choice ... Now, he had a willing listener in the evangelist – in whom, instinctively, he could put his trust.

Soames listened sagely, then, Messiah-like, raised his

119

hand. 'It's not my place to judge – from what I feel – you should go back to Sara, but not yet, not until you're fit enough, the cuts and bruises have healed, and you have a sensible suit of clothes. Certainly, not until the hostility towards you has quietened down. You already know what they're capable of.'

'It's true I should lie low for a while – while I think things out.'

'In the meantime, where will you go?'

'My brother is in America and has invited me. I had wondered about settling there with Sara – but in the meantime… In no circumstances could I return to my home. We live – I lived in Pimlico. I shall have to take a room for a while.'

'No, no, no. I won't have it,' insisted the evangelist with a vigorous shake of the head. You're coming to the mission with me for a while. Give it all a chance to settle down.'

Crigga was far behind him now in miles, but could never be far from his mind and, as he dozed at the back of the van, Wickenham could hear the voice of Sara speaking softly, with passion: '… *fashion the stepping stones to draw me nigh*…' There were tears in her voice and in his eyes.

Now, in the Pemberthy cottage, Sara crouched foetal on her truckle bed, clutching The Wickenham Book of Verse. She started at the sound of Luke's voice. 'Do 'ee have some broth, maid …' She declined and curled further within herself, too stricken to cry.

Reports from coastguard and constable had denied all hope and, in the days to come, gross, insensitive gossip came her way: 'The stranger's body ent been found …' 'Tes been washed up-along, you …' 'He do be gone, the tide got 'un'…'

All the hope in the world was lost to Sara and, as the days and the weeks rolled by, she moved lightly, like a lost soul in drudgery, heedless of Elizabeth's jibes and ill-prophesies. Then, one evening, Pendenna took her aside. She listened and conceded for the coming child's sake – almost unaware of his words.

'I did speak for 'ee afore, maid, and I do speak for 'ee again. I do know 'ee be grieving for the stranger, but he be dead and gone. And I know you do be with child – you be mazed when 'ee cried it out on the headland. The babby needs a father and I am willing to wed 'ee proper...'

Soon, Sara moved uncomprehending, dressed in old lace, as in sacrifice, for the simple wedding. Then, after giving birth to her premature child, she died – drained of life – leaving the tiny mite in the world a virtual orphan.

Then, one autumn evening, Elizabeth was sitting beside the fire, when her eyes glazed over. Suddenly alive with a leap of flame, she sent shockwaves into Luke. 'The stranger do be coming. He do be on his way … He don't know she be dead … Don't let 'un take the babby. Give 'un to Joe. I don't want the bastard no more …'

VISITOR

It was late when Wickenham arrived by the London train. This time he went from the station by stealth. He had no intention of encountering Shaddy Bunt, whose duplicity had caused his near-drowning and separation from Sara, and who would immediately sound the alarm.

The pathway was glittering with frost as he trod nearer, and the cold moon speared the night cloud to light his way… *'the bristling moon – a platinum porcupine of sly delight …'* seeped into his mind as he made his way. Perhaps Sara was quoting his work now – at this moment? He strode with purpose, a mixture of excitement and fear as he neared the Pemberthy cottage. He would argue for her, make them understand that he was the father of her child. He knocked. The squat door opened. Luke raised a lantern and, shining in the light, Wickenham saw the sudden horror etched on the old man's weather-beaten face. 'God's mercy!'

'Yes, I live – with no thanks to Crigga. God *was* merciful to me. And as the father of our child, I have come for Sara. I love her and shall take her and the child away – as far from this place as possible.'

Luke stood stunned at the threshold. Then, quietly, for fear of disturbing Elizabeth who slept fitfully by the fire, 'I do understand – and I do feel right sorry for all that has happened, but …' Events had mellowed Luke and, with tremored voice, he laid a hand on Philip's shoulder and spewed it out. 'I do be right sorry, but the maid be dead.'

'Dead? Sara?' Philip stood stunned, struck in the belly. As he stood there, uncomprehending, Luke thought quickly, loth to give way to a tug-of-war for his premature grandchild. 'And the babby, gone before his time to the good Lord.'

The words struck a fiercer blow. 'Both dead?' he quavered.

'She did grow ill, thinking 'ee drowned.'

A muddle of regret raced through Philip's mind. He should have returned sooner – despite being battered, bruised and raw in enmity. The primal howl caught in his throat gave way to a pained whimper, for he who had knocked at the cottage door with strong resolve, now stood impotent against the night.

'Do 'ee hush! Tent no use now. Best go from Crigga, boy – afore they do scat 'un.' Luke put a sympathetic hand on Philip's shoulder and the door closed.

Numbed, robbed of purpose and direction now, the poet wandered Crigga beyond the night like a lost soul. Yet in his desolation, his mind was beginning to teem with lines of verse. He stood on the headland and looked above the bay. A cluster of stars hung like diamonds that had spilt from the heavens and lingered before they fell. A wonderful image in despair, they suspended him from mundane things, and he had the sudden notion that poets suffer – they *must* suffer and, at that moment, he found his purpose: the Sara sonnets were already conceived and must be born.

Soon he found himself beside the rail track, and followed the route along. An early morning train screamed by, jolting him from his stupor, and he saw that he was approaching the halt. He would catch a train, if he knew where he was going, and wandered cold and exhausted onto the parallel road.

Philip was near to collapse when he saw an inn emerge over the brow, and resolved to take a room – long enough for sustenance and to gather his senses. The inn was not yet open, but he clanged the bell and waited. After a while the heavy door creaked open and the inn keeper stood there, dishevelled and uncomprehending.

'Good morning.'

'What do 'ee want?'

'I wish to take a room.'

'Tes too early for that. Ent open for business, you.'

'But I am cold and exhausted. May I please come in and wait?'

The inn keeper weighed him up and at once softened. 'Cums 'ee in then. You'm frozen to the bone.'

Settled in a nook by the fire, Wickenham grimaced, for barely a flame flickered in the grate.

'Just lit 'un, but it'll draw,' said his host. 'Beth!' he called, hastily scooping up the coins that the guest had tumbled on the table before him, 'A wedge o' bread and cheese and a glass o' wine for the gentleman.'

As the fire began to catch and the logs blaze, Philip, offered a crumb of comfort, still in his greatcoat, slumped in the corner and slept.

It was a welcoming hostelry. So long as the visitors paid their way and behaved themselves, they were left to come and go as they pleased. This suited Philip well, and he decided to rest up there for a few days to recover his strength.

In the quiet of his room at the inn, he knew that he would be able to apply himself to poetry. For many months his pen had been mute. Constantly challenged by Catherine, he had striven in vain, incapable of producing any meaningful verse. Now in the recesses of his mind he sensed sonnets – lines of pentameter carrying rhythms soaring with emotion, as though Sara Michal's sole purpose had been to inspire him. Instinctively, he knew that the Sara sonnets hung in full cloud – to drop gently as snowflakes ready to melt onto the page. Here, while the sleet hammered on the windowpane, he would write far into the night – until his cramped fingers forced him to lay down his pen. Then he would sleep and wake again, disturbed by an imperious muse, who, on such a night, called him to the darkened sky: '*How jealously the wan moon looked on you ...*'

In a few days, Wickenham embarked on a ship bound for San Francisco. From there, he travelled north to America to stay with his brother in Boston where, little by little, the mysterious sonnets were completed, and within a year he had earned world-wide fame.

New York was alive with news of the celebrated young poet from England and the mysterious Sara Sonnets. Soon enough, Jeffries discovered his protégé's fame when the poet's face smiled back at him from a literary article in the Times: 'Damn his eyes!'

But fame meant nothing to Philip. It belonged to Sara. As he read his verse It brought her near to him for, when he wrote, it was as though her spirit delighted as new compositions touched the page: '*Yes, you may go, then there will be / No song, no music rolled down the slant of evening ...*'

Now, in New England, far away from Crigga, the poet put down his pen and looked wistfully from the window. Another autumn had gone; the last flaming leaves had dropped and blown away and, as he turned his eyes to the sky, there came the first flurry of winter snow.

THE BREAD OF TEARS

Early summer, 1887.

Brendin was a small, quiet child, all of four and a half years, with a withdrawn, serious air – rather like a stricken bird that had found itself in a friendly, if alien, cage. Somewhere one sensed a tentative smile awaiting release, but the small miracle rarely happened. The overall impression was of a wide-eyed wonder, perhaps at the illimitable aspect of the view, maybe in puzzlement at finding himself there at all.

He wore an assortment of cast-off clothing, which had been cast off even before the previous owner had inherited it. Shades of the dainty Sara and immaculate Wickenham would have wept for their lost child had they glimpsed him. Crigga wept silently for the shame of the need, for the harsh, searing poverty which made it impossible for families to hold up their heads in the old proud, independent way.

With a gravely alert face the boy scanned the thoughtful procession of tired men as they topped the cliff path and headed in various directions for home. Suddenly he spoke, 'Daddy Joseph be coming.'

Phoebe Tonkin, a practical soul who had already lost two husbands at sea, and hoped for a third, left the prodding of pots on the hearth and hurried across to the window.

'Ess he do be.' She went back to deliver a sharp thrust at a squat pan and sighed in anticipation. 'Ent right for a good Christian man to be living alone, you. Tell 'un that, Brendin. You tell 'un that, won't 'ee, when he do come in?'

'Why, Auntie Phoebe?' He regarded her solemnly, with a child's analytical stare.

'Huh, my dear soul,' muttered Phoebe, exasperated, 'what a boy tes to be sure.' She went into action, 'Then put out they platters, you. Daddy Joe'll be shrammed when he do come in, and nothing again in they nets. Do 'ee be quick, boy.'

Brendin, still dreamy eyed, went to the dresser and took down the three chipped dishes.

'Now the spoons, you,' Phoebe encouraged. And when these had been placed on the freshly scrubbed table, 'Now do 'ee crumb the bread.'

Again, Brendin moved through a phase of the morning ritual. He took the three slices of bread she had already sliced and crumbled them into each of the dishes, all ready now to receive their portions of sustaining soup.

'Bless the boy,' he heard Phoebe say from the far distance, 'Tent good for a child to be without a mother.'

Joe Pendenna walked with weary strides up the path and rough-hewn steps to the cottage. It was as though the pattern of his life was represented by the steep uphill trudge. A mere digit among the statistics of near-destitute fishermen along that coast, his own struggle exemplified them all. He was still – to a large extent – living off the dwindling supplies that had sustained him in steadier days – when the profits from pilchards tided over the less spectacular returns of herring and mackerel. Now, with all the catches failing, the future held nothing – for the fisher must fish, and where there are no fish there is nothing at all. Even if alternative work was available, the tragedy remained of a way of life gone, disrupting an entire community geared for centuries to the toil of the sea.

Why the pilchards had deserted that part of the coast, no-one could certainly say. Some blamed a change in their feeding grounds, others the loss of the minerals that hitherto flowed into the sea from the now equally deserted mines. Others, that the new deep-sea trawlers were breaking up the shoals before they could reach shallower grounds. But few Crigga folk in the drear of those unhappy days doubted that the misfortune had stemmed from the grey house; that disaster had struck and multiplied from the time the very first brick was laid on the headland sanctuary. And it stood now, its sombre shadow still casting a spell towards the people.

An uneasy peace had descended on Crigga, compounded from the fisheries failures and the departure of Jeffries. The drama of Philip and Sara had shocked him, prompting his temporary withdrawal to London – leaving the grey house in the care of security men and faithful Clements. For a while, all was quiet on the headland.

Pendenna, the burden of worry heavily on him as he approached the cottage, nevertheless managed an encouraging wave to the little figure at the window. Joe had never forgotten his vow to look after the boy, but the type of boy the years might produce for him to look after had never crossed his mind. Superficially, the circumstances were not unusual – a motherless boy brought up as another's own. But Brendin was not his own. Joe was obliged increasingly to surrender to that truth as the months went on. And it was not just a matter of crossed Crigga relationships, where a fisherman's child might have passed for another fisherman's child, for Brendin was potently different. Never were parental patterns planted more indelibly on an offspring. He was a good, pleasant looking, obedient boy, but his mind was his own, sacrosanct, always at one remove from established things – as if peering into the world from a universe none other could glimpse.

Far greater philosophers than Joe would have found the situation trying. He was a simple, single channel man with a set outlook and a dislike for complications, yet here he was – inextricably enmeshed in the second generation of the Wickenham web, saddled with the living evidence of the union between the woman he had loved and the man he has hated. What in Brendin was Sara and what Philip Wickenham he couldn't guess, but if only a fingertip had been of the essence of Sara Michal, he would have loved all the boy for the love of that. Brendin sensed this and was fond of Joe, but sadly, through the fault of neither, there could never be a true bond between them.

At last, with a grateful grunt, Joe was at the open door of the cottage, 'How be 'ee, boy? How be 'ee then, Phoebe?'

Phoebe drew her forearm in a sweep across her brow, beady damp from the fumes of the fire, 'The better for seeing 'ee safe. 'How be the fishin' then, Joe?'

'Ent seen more 'n a bucketful o' they toads.' He deposited a small token of his personal labour into a corner, 'Tes fish and tatties for dinner, Brendin boy. Or, if we be lucky, tes tatties and fish.'

'Oh, do 'ee hush,' Phoebe objected, 'Sit 'ee down, you, and drink the hot soup. I've a mind to find 'ee a corner of pasty or two come tonight. Don't 'ee fret, Joe.' She began ladling the soup into the dishes over the crumbled bread, till in a magical, longed for moment, a volcano of liquid savoury pudding erupted from the depths of the plate and bubbled appetisingly before the spoon. 'Begin,' Phoebe ordered, 'but do 'ee watch that it ent too hot for 'ee.'

Soon there was no sound but the sucking of tongue and lip against the scalding soup. Brendin slowly drifted his spoon round the extreme edge of the dish, skimming up tasty clots of the saturated crumbs – blowing on them, sipping them miserly, willing them and praying for them to last. But for all his patient manipulations the tide steadily receded and, eventually, all was forgotten in the dismal sound of the spoon drily scraping against the barren base of the plate. He looked expectantly around, but this morning there were no second helpings. Despite the rough badinage, Phoebe had caught the message on Pendenna's face – the grim need to pare and conserve.

'Off with 'ee, then,' Phoebe said, 'Go out and play, boy, but don't 'ee run off.'

'Ess, watch where 'ee do go or I'll scat 'un, mind,' Joe warned with a kindly glint in his eye.

'Ess, Daddy Joseph.' Brendin looked at them both – the only mother and father figure he was ever likely to know and, with a last wistful glance at the polished dish, slid from his chair and went out of the door. Phoebe watched as he crossed by the window, walking with pathetic dignity for one so young.

'Poor little soul,' she said, with unexpected feeling, 'What's to become of 'un, Joe?'

'What's to become of any o' we, maid?'

'But the child be different. You do know he be different. He ent made for Crigga ways.'

'He do have sense,' Joe countered. 'It'll work out for the boy when 'ee do grow up.'

'No,' Phoebe insisted, 'I do fear for 'un, Joe. It were a good brave thing that 'ee done, but you need a wife, Joe. There be the boy wandering, me widowed, you living alone what's to become of 'un? Where be it going to end?'

'I do thank 'ee, maid, but I ent ever marrying again.'

'Don't it seem more sense, Joe – one nest for all? No need for love in it.'

Joe shook his head gravely, 'Ess, maid. There do be need for some love.' It was a joy he had failed to find. 'There be no home without love.'

Phoebe sighed, 'Tes her, innum?' she said resignedly, 'She be gone, Joe. How don't 'ee take hold o' that?'

'Ess, she be gone, but I got the boy.'

'You ent got the boy.' She turned to challenge him, red streaks of spite suddenly tinging the jealousy she strove to withhold. 'All Crigga knows you ent got the boy.'

He struck the table in anger, 'Do 'ee hush, Phoebe. Do 'ee mind what 'ee say!'

'*No*, you ent got the boy,' she said for the third time, 'He be the grey house, not Crigga, Joe. You'll not hold 'un from there.'

'The grey house be shut,' Pendenna said.

'Eh? Who told 'ee then?'

'Shaddy Bunt.'

'Shaddy? He do know they be sendin' things down from Lunnon.'

Joe grimaced, 'What's this to the boy, maid?'

Phoebe rose and laid a half-caressing hand on his shoulder, '*You* do know. Keep a hold on 'un, Joe, if 'ee can. He be the white crow to Crigga, the white crow from the grey house.'

THE DAY OF THE CHILD

Unaware of the controversy seething around him, Brendin was getting on with the straightforward task of a four-and-a-half-year-old seeking daily adventure. He possessed no toys, but with certain sternly forbidden exceptions, all Crigga and its open spaces were his playground – to be moulded and peopled as his imagination grew. Pools, beaches, headland, wildflowers, insects, and birds – even the dust-engrained coaling schooners – all represented the raw materials from which to weave the magic of dreams.

Most Crigga infants were confined to their backyards, but provided he observed the taboos, Brendin was free to roam during the daylight hours. Indeed, it would have proved a problem to stop him, since wanderlust seemed part of his nature. Fishwives and their men rolled disapproving eyes as he trod by yet came to expect him, but within their ken he was safe.

This early spring morning he picked his way with instinctive care down the shallow cliff terraces that led to the quayside and lower cellars. The latter already reflected the faceless grin of disaster, tar denuded, wood splintered and cracked, the great doors swinging unlocked or mockingly secured by padlocks bearing the rust of disuse. Brendin skipped in and out of one where, cut deep in stone like a waiting sepulchre, it gloomed in the dark with the ghosts of all harvest past, and where the faint aroma of pilchards still lingered.

Brendin went his way, climbing the winding road – up which, in days not known to him, the carts would trundle the fish on route to the inland markets. The top of the road with its junction at Fore Street was significant to Brendin. He loved it as the thoroughfare which led away from Crigga to the station, Truro Road, and all the conjectured mysteries of even more faraway places. Nobody, at Joe's request, ever let the boy turn left towards these distant hazards, so the junction represented a barrier which was much more exciting. Often Brendin would stand enraptured at the dread boundary, to watch the smoke from the station – where the spark and steam-belching monsters were fiery dragons indeed. Then, with a sigh and to the warning glance of passing villager, he would reluctantly turn and make his way back.

But there was an even more awesome reason why that stretch was taboo: the Pemberthy cottage. Luke Pemberthy was alright, of course, and the fisherfolk sympathised with him, but his wife was seen as a witch. The whole village shuddered and whispered it. There were witch-like figures in most rural communities, and poor Elizabeth Pemberthy, in her dotage, centrepiece of village gossip, visited by the curse of the grey house, and driven half-demented by a shame that was now living evidence to the third generation, was an ideal candidate for the title.

Joe had warned repeatedly against going anywhere near the cottage, for at best the old woman was unstable, and on any other day Brendin would have returned as usual along the headland crest, but this morning he was tempted. Gazing as usual towards the forbidden distances, he noticed a group of people mumbling and nodding to each other just beyond the notorious cottage. Infantile experience assured him that gatherings of grown-ups nodding and mumbling meant that something interesting was happening. He hesitated. Then, braced by the courage of curiosity, he forgot all warnings and started off towards them.

To reach the group he must pass the cottage and, as he drew near, a wave of even greater inquisitiveness urged him towards it. Creeping along the shelter of the stone wall, he approached the low gateway tense, his heart almost stopping at the thought of what he might see. He reached the gate, paused for a trembling second, rose on tiptoe to peer quickly over the top, and screamed suddenly at the high strangled shriek.

Elizabeth, aware of the obviously expectant gathering up the road, had ventured out to investigate. Now she stood – figure bent, supported by a stick clasped in gnarled fingers, shoulders draped with an old black shawl, hair wispy white, face wrinkle-webbed, the chin pointed and mobile with secret mutterings. All this Brendin noted with a long thrill of horror, but it was her eyes he remembered most as she swivelled to challenge him – half-mooned in concentration, burning with furious fire that scorched into him. Shrilly, he screamed again and again, while all eyes from the waiting group suddenly turned to the scene.

Then she uttered – not speech but dry croaking, each syllable punctuated by a threatening sweep of the stick. 'Begone, curse 'ee. Begone little bastard – or I won't answer for 'ee.'

The villagers shuffled in awe, each inviting the other to do something and, at last, as Brendin withdrew shaking and sobbing, a woman found the courage to come forward.

'Do 'ee hush, mother Pemberthy,' she admonished, herself pale and shocked by her own bravado, 'Cums 'ee to me boy, let's take 'ee away.'

Brendin was lifted and clasped in strong arms. The old woman turned and retreated, still cursing and shaking the stick, and it was Luke who appeared in the doorway, disturbed from his rest and laden with worry, to usher her finally inside. Brendin, shaken but soothed, was set down and would have run home, but at that moment a cry went up from the watchers: 'They be coming. Here they do be!'

Round the bend from the direction of the Truro Road came the first rumble and then the sight of a huge pantechnicon, clearly intended for the grey house – since no other dwelling in Crigga could possibly have accommodated its contents. On it came, drawn by four horses, the driver perched on its flimsy seat and concentrating his energy on the testing task of containing the clumsy vehicle within the limits of the rough narrow road. As it passed with its rear flap open, Brendin could see other men inside, sitting and swaying on mounds of cases and furniture. The group, like a cluster of sheep, made way and silently fell in behind, Brendin among them, and slowly the procession continued to the last stage to the grey house.

Brendin, recovering now from his fearful confrontation with Elizabeth, and becoming guiltily aware that he was in the process of exchanging one great taboo for another, now broke from the crowd. He ran instead to a little eyrie he knew – at the rim of a hollow not far from the Huer's Hut, where he could watch safely without being observed. He had no means of knowing that Jeffries had now decided to risk re-opening his fortress in the hope that Crigga animosity had died down.

Brendin knew, from Joe, that he must never go near the grey house, that this mysterious place was the cause of all Crigga's misfortune. That it contained a dragon he was quite certain. By what other means could such harm have been wrought among the villagers? And someone lived there who might well be another witch. He had glimpsed her once. And a grocer's cart came often with provisions. Perhaps they brought food for the dragon? Were they going to take the dragon away?

So does a child's mind weave and drift through the

flood of its day, its surface a frail sop to reality – its depths a teeming universe of wonder, invention, and delight. But for all his watchfulness there came no dragon, and there was no conflict today – just the torturous manoeuvring of the pantechnicon through the outer gateway of the grey house, and a few hisses and jeers from the crowd as it disappeared inside. And then, nothing. He could make out the high roof of the wagon looming above the walls, but that was all. The crowd still lingered in a token of Crigga disapproval, but the cutting edge of their hostility had been blunted by time.

By the time Brendin had fulfilled his vigil, pensively propped against the tingling pillow of headland grasses, it was mid-afternoon. There would be no point in going home. Daddy Joseph would not yet be up. And the beaches called. The tide was now almost fully out, with smooth golden sand in a semi-circle embracing promontory and cove. This was his favourite playground of them all, where stones smoothly round were there for the picking, to be flung and plopped into the pools, where the pools were unchartered deeps, the shrimps and mallards, monstrous denizens of the ocean, and empty mussel shells voyaged across endless spaces to fabulous lands beyond – even the ken of Davey and the Katie full of coal. Each cavern harboured potential gryphons, and imagination traced grotesque beings wherever the shadows grew.

With a wave to the stranded Katie from the harbour, he rounded the jetty on the seaward side and dabbled in the newly revealed secrets of an unusually low tide. Wandering aimlessly without thinking, he suddenly looked round with a guilty twinge – leavened with excitement and fear. He was within yards of breaking the third and greatest taboo of them all.

The cove lay innocently quiet in a ray of sunshine, its

sides crag-toothed and ominously threatening even in the mild spring day. Ahead of it, past the out-jut of tell-tale rock, the cavern loomed. For a second the boy held back, but taboo often feeds curiosity till it becomes stronger than the taboo and, drawn by a force beyond reason, and after a hurried look round, he began inching his way carefully across the stones, round the big boulder, and on to the cavern mouth. Then, with a huge gulping breath, he entered the cave.

It was gloomily dark in there, but he could see that it went around and back on itself. He continued inwards, breathing quickly, till all was blackness before him and only the faintest glimmering showed at the entrance behind.

He paused, intending to turn back, but with a little flutter of fear seemed unable, as though something indescribable was holding him there. A silence crept in that was more than a silence. The darkness was pitch, darker than the dark, and he felt his gaze directed hypnotically to the further recesses of the cave. The profound silence held for a while, though distant voices seemed trying to break through. The blackness grew even blacker, vibrations trembled, half-formed, dissolved, took vague, shimmering shape till his eyes closed against the impossible, and he re-opened them to glimpse a distant figure, and to hear his own whimper of sobbing that rose and merged into plaintive words. 'Boy! Brendin!' A hail from the outer world suddenly broke in on the enchantment. 'Where be 'ee, boy? What's to do there?'

At last, Brendin managed to turn around. The grey bulk of Dan Bicknell stood there, framed in the dim light of the entrance. 'What be doing, boy? Are 'ee mazed?' he said, 'How don't 'ee come over here?'

In a daze, as though making from sleep, Brendin obeyed. Bicknell, with a mild scolding, gathered him up and hurried back to the open. 'Good thing I saw 'ee. Mustn't ever go in there,' he chided. Daddy Joe told me, and I be telling 'ee. Tide'll catch 'ee, else.'

'Mister Bicknell …'

'Ess, boy. Ess?'

Brendin looked at him with solemn enquiry, 'What about the other man? Won't the tide catch him, too?'

Dan Bicknell halted, studying his charge curiously, 'Bless 'ee, boy. Which man? Ent no other man,' he said, puzzled.

'Ess there be,' Brendin insisted, 'In the cave. I did hear him – just before you came in.'

'Do 'ee hush, Bicknell said, 'I didn't hear nothing.' His tone held a quiver in it. 'Now step out sharp, you. We be going to Daddy Joe.'

But the child had sensed something, attuned to the fourth dimension. Not Wickenham, as many had whispered, but a concentration of negative vibrations, one desperate imprint upon many imprints born of the terror of drowning in the cove.

'Do 'ee tell all,' Joe said. He had just risen, heavy-eyed, ready to prepare for another unpromising night, when Dan and the boy came in. 'What's to do, Dan?' he asked.

Briefly, Dan retailed the doings of the day – the arrival at the grey house, Brendin's encounter with Elizabeth, the tailing of him to the cave, the boy's uncanny remark … 'I do tell 'ee this,' he concluded, 'for the good o' the boy. Ent no business o' mine, but 'ee do need looking after – roamin, around like 'ee do.'

'Ess,' Joe agreed, 'Ent no business of yours, Dan, but I do thank 'ee proper. I'll be seeing to 'un.'

'The boy be tired, Joe,' Bicknell insisted, 'Like as not 'ee nodded off. He's been hearin' things.'

'I do thank 'ee,' Joe said again. When the fisherman

had gone, he looked wearily at Brendin, a small light in his darkness. 'Do all this be so, boy?'

Brendin answered tensely, 'Ess, Daddy Joseph.'

'And didn't I tell 'ee? Didn't I tell 'ee what I'd do to 'ee?'

'Ess, Daddy Joseph.'

'This talk, in the cave. You did have a dream, boy. Do 'ee understand?'

Brendin was silent.

'Do 'ee *understand*?'

'Ess, Daddy Joseph - but it weren't a dream.'

Joe began undoing the heavy leather belt that he wore. Brendin squirmed on his low chair, his face pale and expectant.

'Come 'ee here,' said Joe. Brendin hesitated, then slowly rose.

'Don't scat 'un, Joe!' Phoebe stood in the doorway, bearing a pasty, 'The boy did have enough. His ways ent like our ways. The Lord save the poor lamb.' Tipping her burden onto the table she crossed to Brendin, and for the second time that day he felt close in a woman's arms with a nameless longing, until she eased him away. 'A corner of pasty, then I'll put 'ee to bed,' she said.

'Didn't mean harm to the boy,' Joe explained.

'No, no, bless 'ee, I do know. Come, sit 'ee to the table.'

The pasty was large and hot. There were mere traces of meat in it, but a savoury chopping of onion, and plenty of juice-soaked potato, gave it bulk.

'Lord, reward our labour, and send the nets in with a blessing. Amen,' they mumbled together.

Phoebe tucked Brendin up in the truckle bed that was retained in the inner room, and where later she would also sleep till Pendenna was due to return. Then she bustled back to the kitchen.

'Auntie Phoebe?'

'Do 'ee go to sleep, boy.'

'But Auntie Phoebe …'

'Ess?'

His words came dreamily, 'I really *did* hear another man in the cave.' There was a long silence. The wind rustled dry creeper leaves against the outer glass of the window. A night bird chuckled in unison with the weird shadows twisting along the cliff-side wall.

'Do 'ee hush, boy,' she said fearfully, 'You do know that be nonsense.' Then, in scared contradiction, as she crossed nervously to the comforting splutter of the fire, 'What do 'ee mean, then? What did 'ee say?'

Brendin yawned on the edges of sleep. 'He did say, 'Sara… Sara…'

MEETING

Uncle Jeffries played his cards carefully on his return to Crigga. He came in weary hope of finding something of the peace and tranquillity of which he felt Philip Wickenham had deprived him. He understood that there was little chance of an armistice but was determined not to offend the villagers if he could possibly avoid it, and there was no great eruption – only the occasional tremor.

One of his first tasks was to re-instate Shaddy Bunt, a somewhat doubtful move, for Shaddy had long forfeited any respect he might have enjoyed previously. His ploy for revenge had been held in contempt by the basically fair fishermen. However, Jeffries knew nothing of that, and the discredited Bunt was ushered back. Still irrepressibly adept at snapping up what he could, he was thankful to be within permissible reach of a full kitchen and Clements' pasties.

The comings and goings at the grey house remained a source of interest to Brendin and, soon after he had seen the pantechnicon arrive on that eventful day, he again wandered to the headland with infant curiosity – fed by the taboo. He sat on the grass, pulling the blades carefully apart as he searched for little creatures, entering their busy worlds. Contemplating all things natural, he looked up to the sky, wondering whether – if he got a box or a ladder – it would be possible to touch it? As he thought this, he caught a glimpse.

It was a strange glimpsing. He had closed his eyes for a moment against the hot sun and, when he re-opened them, there she was – suddenly in view at the far end of the high circular wall surrounding the house. She could not possibly have covered the distance from the main gate in the time, and where else she could have come from was a mystery. One second, she was gone. The next, she was filling his vision like a pisky – magically materialising from an enchanted wood.

He stared, utterly fascinated by an arrival so completely in contrast with the usual procession of monotone adults. Indeed, skipping lightly across the pink-strewn turf, she might easily have been a fairy – dainty with ribbons in her hair, and dressed in what to Brendin was an outrageous Sunday best of colours and frills. Perhaps he was dreaming after all, for there were enough bewitchments and goblins and piskies in Crigga to make it probable at least. He closed his eyes again, putting it to the test. When he re-opened them a few seconds later she was still there – looking in his direction. He closed his lids once more, screwed them tight, forcing himself to count slowly up to ten, then opened them quickly. This time she had disappeared.

He waited and waited, but she failed to re-materialise, and he was enrapt with the conundrum for the next few days. She had certainly not come or gone through the great gate, which lay to the far left of his observation, and she couldn't have climbed over the high wall. He was a discerning boy, and the only possible answer, if indeed she was not a sprite, seemed to lie in the presence of a second door round the hidden side of the wall. Brendin shuddered at the mere thought of this. In all his life he had only scanned the grey house from afar, and had never yet dared to set foot on the further headland, or venture into the unknown territory of absolute taboo. But now, for all his inner dread, temptation gripped and overcame him. He would, *must*, go down and explore beyond the visible wall.

On the third morning after his unusual sighting, he crept cautiously out from his concealing hollow and, with fluttering heart, began the hazardous journey across his familiar stretch of headland towards the forbidding wall. Reaching it, and taking care to keep close within its sheltering height, he continued slowly round the perimeter. Looking backwards and upwards, he saw he was now out of sight of the Huer's Hut and the hollow, and must therefore be at last, what was to him, on completely untrodden soil. He paused, a little surprised to find that, after all, everything in the banned area – the headland itself, the sound of the sea, the sky, the carpeting turf, were the same here as anywhere else. There were no wizards, no visible dragons, no weird outlandish sights at all.

Emboldened, he resumed his circuit of the great outer wall, and there, sure enough, was a sturdy green gate set solidly into the stonework. *This* must be the means of exit and entry – skipping round the wall briefly and back again. Like most mysteries, the solution was clear when common-sense had been found.

He sat on the turf in the proud flush of adventurous achievement, then, with a sudden surge of bravado tempered with fear, went slowly across, and placed an exploratory hand on the door. He pushed, very slightly, and it began to move inwards. Then, without any warning, it was flung back fully, and he found himself staring awe-struck at an accusing face peering demandingly at him from his own level.

'What *are* you doing, boy?' she asked in a cross whisper, 'You mustn't come in here.' Putting a finger to her mouth to urge silence, she closed the door quietly and beckoned him to a spot out of sight of it. Then, with imperious confidence, she began an interrogation. 'Who *are* you, boy?'

Brendin could only stare, as one tends to do in the face of small miracles, taboos and punishments and eerie visitations forgotten. He had never seen anyone as delectably pretty in his life. Her features were well-formed and piquant, with forthright, enquiring brown eyes. Her hair was in ringlets tied back with a ribbon, her frock a mass of flounces and frills. Her hands were dominantly propped on her hips as she stood challenging him. 'Well, boy,' what *is* your name?'

He stood in poverty – rough contrast – ragged, clean, his face polished with Phoebe's brisk work with a flannel. At last, he managed to speak, 'I be Brendin.'

'*Brendin*? Oh, that's a funny name. Where are you from?'

'Crigga.' The word was all-embracing for him.

'You mean the village? Oh, that awful place.'

'Tent awful,' he retorted, gathering courage, 'Not like the grey house.'

'Oh, what's wrong with the Greywalls?'

Foolishly, he suddenly realised that he had no direct evidence of *anything* wrong.

'There be a dragon in it,' he said.

'There *be*,' she mocked, 'There *be* a dragon! What about the village, then? They threw stones at the house, and broke it all up.'

'Only to kill the dragon,' he countered, 'And it weren't me.'

'Oh, no, it *weren't* you,' she mimicked, 'and they didn't kill the dragon either, you silly boy. 'Cos there wasn't a dragon.'

'There were.'

'No there wasn't.' She revised her line of attack. 'Why were you spying on me?'

'I weren't.'

'Yes, you *were*.'

'I did only try to look in the door.'

'No, before that. You spy from up there.' She waved her arm. 'I've seen you from the nursery window. You

144

spy all day long.'

'Ent spying, just looking,' he said.

'Why?'

He didn't answer directly. He looked at her, and said at last, 'Tes proper up there. How don't 'ee come – and play with me?'

'Play with *you*?' She mimed shocked refusal, but was clearly undecided. 'No, I can't. I can only play here by the house.'

'I ent allowed to come here,' he said.

'Coward, then – cowardy, cowardy custard,' she jibed.

'No I ent. If I be, *you are.*'

'Silly…'

'Hannah! Hannah!' an authoritative female voice suddenly broke in from somewhere the other side of the wall, 'Hannah! Where be to? Come in this moment!'

'Oh, dear,' Hannah sighed with a toss of the curls, 'that's Clements and she'll be *mad* …' She scampered away in a flurry of frills. Then stopped and turned. 'If you're not cowardy custard, come tomorrow,' she said.

But the next day it rained, and all he could do was nurse his frustration at home, following the trickles as they slid in dreary procession down the window. The third day he scampered eagerly to the rendezvous and she failed to appear. But on the fourth morning, he was relieved to see her creep stealthily from the door.

'That Clements,' she complained witheringly, 'said the ground was too wet to go out. Sit down, boy. Talk to me.'

'Who be Clements, then?'

'*Who's Clements*? She looked at him with unfeigned astonishment, '*Everybody* knows Clements.'

'I don't.'

'Clements looks after me. And she looks after all

145

Greywalls.'

'Phoebe do look after me,' he said. 'Do Clements be your mummy?'

'No, silly. Of course not. My mummy is ill. She's always ill. Is yours?'

'Ent got no mummy,' he said, 'only Phoebe.'

They looked at each other in silence, instinctively savouring the common ache of deprivation. Then she changed the subject abruptly. 'You *are* funny, aren't you?'

'I ent.'

'There you are. *Ent.* Why do you say ent when you mean I'm not?'

He tried to hit back but could not, responding too naturally to the fascination of her, a friend even more intriguing than Welsh Davey who brought coal in the schooner, who gave him cake and called him Boyo.

'I'm *not*, then,' he conceded, and this was the gentle beginning of a permeating influence she was thereafter to have on him, imperceptibly moulding him to her ways. She smiled, sensing the conquest, and turned to snuggle down on the warm springy turf.

Gradually, they grew close – chattering, arguing, smoothing the bobbing pinks, parting the grasses to probe the worlds of tiny scurrying creatures, sharing the fantasies that come alive in the wondrous universe of the child, till the grave little Brendin found himself crowing with the first real laughter he had known.

They were safe in the lee of the further wall, for few people had inclination or cause to venture to the rear of the grey house, and the favoured spot was out of sight of the village heights. Yet inevitably, as the days went by and the forbidden magic of Crigga beckoned, restlessness grew.

'How don't 'ee come up to the cliff, then?' Brendin

suggested one afternoon, when limited play had been exhausted and Hannah was gazing wistfully towards the upper headland.

'What? *Why* don't *you*,' she corrected, 'You know I can't. I mustn't ever go anywhere near the village.'

'Cliff ent – *isn't* – the village.' He pointed upwards in the direction of the hidden hollow, 'Tes nice up there. Ent – *Isn't* – no-one to see 'ee.'

'I can't.'

'Cowardy, then.'

'I'm *not*.'

'You be. Come on, then.'

Such a challenge, with any excuse waiting to be snatched at, could have only one outcome, 'Alright, I'll race you,' she said.

The hollow lay warm and secret, full baited for the sun and. for a while, the two drowsed in peace, lazily chatting. But adventure breeds from itself, and Brendin was to have a further reminder of his weird heritage that afternoon.

Soon, Hannah became fidgety and took a few tentative steps towards the seaward ridge – beyond which tumbled the downward slope of the cliff edge.

Brendin sat up. 'Don't go there!' he warned.

'Why not?' She was defiant.

'Tes the cove down there. That be where people get dead. They do fall into the sea.'

'People? What people?' Her voice tried to mock, but she was uncertain and halted.

'People,' said Brendin, 'and there be a man down there.'

This time she laughed. Even from where she stood, the hissing thunder of breakers against the grim teeth of the inlet was audible. 'A man, silly boy? Down there? How can there be?'

'There *must* be a man down there,' he insisted stubbornly.

'Alright, then. Let's look over and see him.'

'Don't 'ee do it,' he pleaded, deeply scared, 'Do 'ee come back, Hannah.'

'Cowardy,' she said.

'No, I ent. I don't want 'ee to fall.'

'Come with me, then.' She turned, and, half sitting, began inching across the slope. 'I'm going to look,' she said.

Brendin, fearful for her safety, climbed from the hollow and cautiously slid after her, calling for her to return. Somehow, he reached her and tried pulling her back, but though she gripped his hand tightly, she taunted him till he was forced to continue.

'I thought you said he was there. Show me the man,' she demanded.

It was a perilous exercise. The incline fell away gently at first, punctuated by turf humps and sizeable stones, then dipped more sharply to the ultimate edge where, from the tumbled scree and sparse grasses space, descended dizzily to the rocks awash two hundred feet below. The children lowered themselves by breath-taking degrees, making use of whatever handholds there were. Brendin's heart drummed, yet he felt drawn by the intense magnetism that always came into force whenever he strayed within distance of the cove.

They dug their heels to a timorous halt, forced to stop because one further step would have plummeted them into empty air. Hannah tried to lean forward, clawing at Brendin for support, and they clung to each other tightly as she peered abortively into the void.

'I – can't – see – anything,' she gasped, 'Brendin, we'd better go back.'

But now it was Brendin who refused to move, meshed

in the web of the mysterious influence whose intangible threads would not let him go.

'I'm afraid,' Hannah breathed tremblingly, 'I want to go back.'

'No, I be going to look,' he said tensed.

'You can't. You can't see anything.'

'Ess I can – if I do turn around.'

Horrifically, he swivelled on the edge of the precipice, till his head hung over, to get a direct view of the cliff-base, leaving Hannah fearfully gripping the loose grasses and whispering in protest. For a few seconds, Brendin became lost to everything – all his being concentrated on the focal point of the distant cove and the swirling waters. The mist thrown up from the tossing spray seemed to writhe in a tenuous essence, whose beckoning strands had, years before, entranced and inveigled the fated Wickenham.

'Brendin! Brendin!' He heard Hannah call as from a long way off, but he was powerless to respond. Then he shuddered and drooped and, shivering with the twin tears of the known and inexplicable, Hannah at last coaxed and almost dragged him up the slope and back to the safety of the ridge.

The escapade chastened Brendin, reverting him for days to his solemn, grave little self. The children returned often to the hollow, a location nicely balanced between the two great taboos of the village and Greywalls, but never again that summer did they venture to the precipice overlooking the cove. Yet the adventure bequeathed them a bond and an understanding that remained with them for many years to come.

August went by in a new-found tranquillity, and then one dull September morning as he peered from the rim of the lofty hollow, he saw her leave in the jingle, surrounded by luggage.

She turned and waved and he buried his head in the screening grasses. Boys never cry, but he was fearful that even from the lower road she might look up and see him doing it. It was as though she was being drawn from him on a long-spun thread – a strand growing thinner and thinner as the jingle disappeared into the distance, yet still magically held in the mind. He was too young to appreciate such imagery. All he knew was that Hannah had gone. As he hid his eyes in a ragged forearm, she would never know that he wept.

TRANSITION

Time sculpted, and Crigga – village and villagers – were
malleable under the years, shaped by the remorseless
hammers of circumstance. There had to be change, as the
ancient patterns of life steadily dissolved. The old
triumphant cry, 'The fish be coming!' was now a dirge,
'The fish ain't be coming, no more is the cry Hevva!' The
great seine nets were rotting, the cellars in permanent
disuse, the fisherfolk, on the brink of destitution, barely
surviving. Fish there were for the table, and shellfish in
season, but the industry, that for centuries had given
sustenance and character to the place and its people, was
no more.

Yet already destiny was revealing a new
compensation, and towards the end of the century Crigga
was casting nets and eyes at a strange new species
beginning to drift in from the far horizon: visitors. The
era of mass holidaymaking, trippers, and the anonymity
of cemented promenades was still generations distant,
and grandeur for a while remained ungobbled fodder for
the compilers of guidebooks, but the shadows were there.
The railway – a lance driven into the remote Crigga limb,
bore the germs of slow development.

The transition was slow, only to be recognised in
retrospect, and in between there was much heartburning
and distress. Pendenna was a typical case, trying to live
on what little was left from the fat of the pilchards and
what he could glean from the ever-thinning harvest of
herring and mackerel. His cottage was too tiny for
visitors, his boat deteriorating for need of replenishment
and repair. Yet still he resisted stubbornly any departure
from the old rhythms of life.

'Tes fish for breakfast, fish for supper and rags to

wear,' Phoebe complained, 'How don't 'ee take some o' they toads out in the boat with 'ee, Joe? They'll pay good money for 'un.'

'Do 'ee hush, woman.'

'Pascoes be doin' 'un.'

'And I ent,' Joe declared wearily.

All the old folk had died as the old customs and industry had died – the Pemberthys, Trebilcock and Burt. A few, like the Pascoes, had kow-towed to the visitors and accepted coin for abortive sessions of fishing or trips round the bay. But he wouldn't stoop so low, even when, in his deepest troughs of depression, he saw the distant vision of normal contentment evermore receding.

'And the boy,' Phoebe insisted, 'What's to become of the boy?'

'The boy?' The boy was an enigma, not to be fathomed at all. He had tried. Tried to teach him, to bring him up into Crigga ways, to mould him into the craft of boatmanship, fishing for the few that were still to be caught but, though quietly obedient, Brendin was mentally elsewhere. There was no point of contact between them but one, and that was smothered, unmentionable, though daily the stamp of Sara and Wickenham on Brendin's face tortured the simple fisherman.

'He do be seeing that maid,' he said in glum reverie, 'Be *that* what's to become of 'un?'

'I did tell 'ee,' Phoebe said, 'years agone. He do belong to the grey house, scat 'un or no. Face up to 'un, Joe.'

'Who be the maid?' It was a question he had asked almost daily without satisfactory reply, but none knew the comings and goings at the grey house – except, perhaps, Shaddy. But Shaddy was now far gone in the depths of his cups, and at best could only name names.

152

'She do be James. Hannah James, Shaddy do say, and that be all I do know,' Phoebe told him, 'and 'ee won't stop 'un, Joe. The curse of the grey house be on 'un both, and it ent done with yet. Not by a long way, Joe.'

Pendenna rose stolidly and eased past her as she thrust a clumsy iron at a deep sprawling of clothing. For a moment he wanted the nearness of her, and reassurance of a flesh and mind that he knew, the soothing of understanding and sympathy. Then again, he retreated into the inner, unspoken purgatory that had been with him through the years and uttered only from tongue and lips, 'Do 'ee hush, woman.' But there was no hush in his heart as he trod slowly back to the harbour.

Brendin was thirteen at the time of the incident, undergoing his own small trials in the village schoolroom. The schoolmaster, who they called Methuselah, was in the rear guard of those failed academics retreating before the onset of Education Committees and Board Schools, who still, for a pittance of pennies strove to inject the three Rs into heads full of fishing and boats, or crammed with nothing at all, opted to remain that way. The arithmetic was basic, the reading and writing based almost entirely on the Bible, from which simple texts and messages were laboriously scratched out on slates. Though the teaching was drear, Brendin accepted it avidly, thrilled to discover that the acquisition of letters was the potential key to so many doors of understanding. While others lagged, he pressed on, perfecting his new-found instrument whenever he could. Opportunities were few. Joe had no books on view, except a very worn Bible, but from this, Brendin painfully learned poetry, philosophy, and ancient history. If what he read was contradictory, it served to sharpen his mind.

His questions soon out-ran the tired brain of Methuselah, who asked little more than that a fidgeting, undemanding class should scratch uncomprehendingly away at the psalms or sermon on the mount.

'Sir,' Brendin would ask, 'why, if it is wrong to take more than one wife, was Solomon wise?' But this sort of query only earned his detention, the Beatitudes squeaking out again from the impact of pencil on slate.

Today he was able to get away when the class dismissed. The handful of other boys went off to play or to help their fathers down in the harbour. He did not go with them – not that he was deliberately aloof. There was little he could do in uneasy alliance with Daddy Joseph, and a tacit understanding of difference was understood by all – except for a few jeering roughs like the young Pascoes. They were used to him wandering from games to scuff his feet idly in the sand or stare absently out to sea, and would shout, 'Grey house! Grey house!' after him when they saw him straying that way.

But this afternoon, he had a special mission to fulfil if he could pluck up enough courage to venture it. Something Hannah had unwittingly put in his mind, daring and challenging.

Only yesterday, Hannah had gone back after a brief Easter holiday, and he still smarted from the pain of parting. He could not put a name to his feelings. All he knew was that she spelled contentment, grew more lovely each time he saw her and, that when she went, she took a pervading essence of happiness with her. With every goodbye he felt the emptiness within emptiness, an exclusion from the inner temple of being. The last time she had left, she had kissed him – a sudden, shy schoolgirl token, but now he thought she must remain his forever.

In his reverie he had strayed once more to the hollow,

the venue for generations of shattered promises and dreams. He recalled with a shudder their infantile escapade to the crest of the cove, and his certainty that someone constantly called out from the vicinity of the cave.

The fantasy would always be with him, but now his thoughts were all for the absent Hannah, who, more than nine years ago, had skipped into sight from the grey house like a sprite, and had haunted him ever since. The intervening period had been vibrant with laughter and a few tears – with arguments, quarrels, making up, and memorable adventures. He remembered a day when she had enticed him through the garden gate and into the house itself. 'Don't you *dare* tell Clements, Shaddy,' she ordered Shaddy, who had drifted from slumber under a sheltering tree to surprise the intruders, but Shaddy had been thankful enough to retreat and resume his nap. Then she had let Brendin through to the inner shrine of carpeted rooms and library, where deep armchairs and endless rows of books had overwhelmed him. Though not nearly so much as Clements, who had materialised in an aura of wrath.

'So, *this* be the boy?'

'He's a very nice boy,' Hannah had argued.

'Ess, ess, maybe he be. But don't 'ee ever bring 'un in the house again, or the master Jeffries will chop his head off. Now be off with 'ee both. And boy, get back to the village.'

Later, from the lee of the wall, he had glimpsed Jeffries – a big, bluff man who carried an umbrella rather than an axe to chop little boys' heads off. Yet even from a safe distance, it was an awesome experience.

His courage, not yet screwed to the point of positive action, Brendin rose and strolled to a vantage point overlooking the quay, for there was a rumour that the

Katie was due in, and he was anxious to greet his old friend, Davey, who delivered the coal and shared his sandwiches. But the vessel had not arrived. For a space he stood perched on a knoll, gazing towards the further bastions of the bay. Up here he was content with his world, and no developer would ever be able to concrete over the grand sweep of the Crigga he adored, the ocean he loved... To the fishermen it was the necessary anvil on which to fashion their trade, to him a living entity of challenge and desire. He loved the cliffs, the soar of gulls dwelling in them, and inland the meadows and primrose lanes. These brought separate raptures, but there were times when all things blended into a composite beauty that raised and flooded him with the inarticulate poetry of the mind. Then he would pause and wonder in the fastnesses of inspirations he sensed but was unable to express, uplifted and saddened together, for there was so much to see and to be said.

He moved from the knoll, a lonely but rapt little boy, and made his way to the opposite flank of the headland, past the old harbour, and paused by the track that led over the sand dunes to the estuary. This was the path taken by Sara and Wickenham to Sam Chegwidden at Pennan, and where Joe had lately begun to send Brendin with the occasional token bounty of fish. Now the prospect was deserted, except for a vehicle that had been halted where the end of the road back to the village tapered to a churned-up mass in the sand.

It was a cart after the style of a gypsy caravan, though more solid, and with a strong, patient horse between the shafts. The sides of the van bore a series of Biblical portrayals and the text: *Trust in the Lord.* By the side of the horse stood a man – dressed in a serge semi-uniform and a peaked cap. Brendin looked at him curiously, for he had seen no-one like this in Crigga before.

The man, tall, side-whiskered and with a kind, intelligent face, returned the glance with a woe-begone twinkle.

'Bless you son. Is this right for Pennan?'

'Yes,' said Brendin, 'but not for a horse and cart.'

The evangelist looked at him keenly, 'Where are you from, boy? Not the village?'

'Yes, sir, I am.'

'Ah,' he continued to study Brendin, who stood there fresh-faced and serious. 'Where's the Pennan Road, then?'

'It be – is back yonder. Tes a long way round. There's no way of crossing the estuary.'

'Will you come with me and show me?'

'I'm sorry, sir,' In the absence of Hannah, Brendin dropped back a little into the Crigga idiom, 'I ent allowed.'

'Oh, come on, son. No-one will know.'

'Oh, ess, I will,' Brendin said gravely.

The evangelist drew closer. 'Dear God, the boy means what he says. Where did you learn such honesty?'

'Learn? Tes only what's right,' Brendin said.

'Yes, yes, of course. Though all of us don't follow that path. What's your name, boy?'

'Brendin, sir, Brendin Pendenna.'

The evangelist held out his hand, 'I'm Soames. Captain Soames. I travel the roads whenever I can – trying to carry the word. Well, Brendin, will you then *point* out the way?'

Brendin obliged. 'You be staying in Crigga at all, sir?'

For the night, perhaps. But I'm heading for Pennan church. And the fair. Do you go to the big Pennan fair?'

'No, sir. Not yet.'

'Ah, then you can't tell me.' He sized Brendin up once more. 'How about some cake and a quick lemonade.

Would that be allowed?'

'Thank 'ee, sir. I think so, sir.'

Soames led the way to the rear of the van. Inside it was like a ship's cabin – with bunk, table, a tiny stove, and shelves massed with books spaced around the walls. The cake sent Brendin's juices squirming, the lemonade was nectar, never tasted before. Soames watched him carefully. 'You were hungry, boy.'

Brendin was everlastingly hungry, in body and mind, but he didn't say so, 'Yes, sir. Thank you very much, sir.'

The knife made an encouraging second and third sawing sounds into the cake. 'Here, boy. Eat it all up. There, boy. There's an appetite for you, eh?

'Ess, sir. Thank 'ee, sir.'

The cake being now a mass of crumbs, which Brendin's eyes still traced lingeringly over the plate, Soames took down a large Bible.

'A text for me and a text for the road,' he said, 'Blessed are the meek, Brendin. And the pure in heart.'

'Amen,' Brendin said.

You read the Bible, Brendin?'

'Ent nothing else to read, sir.'

'Nothing?'

'No, sir.'

'No storytellers? No poets? Though, of course, the Bible has plenty of those.'

'Nothing, sir.'

'The Psalms are poetry, you know: *Unto thee lift I up mine eyes, O thou that dwellest in the heavens.* Not rhyme, but poetry. You understand that?'

'Ess, sir. I think so, sir.'

'Good. Good boy. You had a poet in Crigga once – Wickenham. Yes, yes. He was – It was *thought* he was drowned here you know. In one of the coves. You know about that?'

'No, sir, but lots of people get drowned.'

Soames sighed. 'True, true. But this was a fine poet in the prime of his life. Sometimes the ways of the Lord are indeed strange.' He reached to the shelf, searching. 'Hm. Wordsworth, Tennyson – thought Wickenham was here. Never mind. I shall come again, Brendin, and you shall have a copy. I must depart now, boy,' said Soames. 'Oh, and – if you should ever need it – here's my card.'

'Oh, thank you sir.' And as the caravan rumbled off, he was left with an address in London smudged in ink – a souvenir from a very happy encounter.

CHANCE

As Brendin made his way to the headland, he suddenly recalled a conversation with Hannah. 'Shaddy,' she had confided in him, 'is becoming *quite* impossible. He doesn't begin to cope with the gardening and all the things he should. Poor old man. He just can't, I suppose.'

'How don't – *Why* don't you get somebody else?'

'Oh, Brendin,' she chided, 'as if you didn't know. Whoever will come to work at Greywalls? There's a dragon there, isn't there? You told me so yourself.'

It was true. Shift for the neutral visitors they might at a pinch, but tradition dies slowly, and though the grey house stood more as a symbol than a threat, no true Crigga soul would ever work for the enemy.

'Poor Clements,' Hannah had mourned, 'She is at her wits' end. All the weeds are growing and there's the planting to do. And Uncle Jeffs will be down in a week or two.'

That same morning Brendin had watched Daddy Joe carefully release a precious penny for the schoolmaster and silently refuse the large helping of soup and bread in the boy's favour. Brendin, if without words, felt deeply for Joe – always so kind so forgiving. It seemed to him that if Joe needed money, and the grey house wanted work done, then a mutual solution might be possible. If he could just steel himself to ask …

Braving the gate and the forbidding drive, he knocked on the front door and stood like a latter-day Oliver – not asking for more, but for any thin droplet of gruel that might be bestowed on him. After a while the door came open and Clements appeared. She had not been face-to-face with Brendin for years and stared at him unbelievingly.

'Dear soul,' she muttered, 'it do be. It do be …' Then, slowly recovering, addressed him directly. 'What be doing here? What be after, boy?'

'I do want …' he quavered.

'Do 'ee go to the side door,' she interrupted, 'This ent no place for the likes of 'ee.

'Ess, missus.' He drew deep breaths to retain his courage and, when the kitchen door opened to him, 'I do want work, ma'am. Doing a bit in the garden.'

'Oh, *do* 'ee, then. And what makes 'ee think…'

'It were Hannah,' he said, 'Hannah did say.'

'Miss James,' Clements rebuked, 'Where are your manners, boy?'

They were there. They were based on Hannah's which were impeccable. But if this was refinement, he accepted it – in the name of the grey house.

'Miss James, then, missus. She did say there were work to do.'

'And where did you see Miss James?'

'On the headland,' he said, trapped.

Clements nodded sternly. 'Boy,' she reproved, 'you will *not* see Miss James. Tent proper 'ee should. Tent proper at all. Now, do 'ee understand that?'

'Ess missus. Yes, ma'am,' said Brendin, abashed and awaiting the final dismissal. He made a last attempt. 'We be poor, ma'am. And Daddy Joe don't get enough to eat.'

Clements spared little time on laughter or tears, but she knew most of his story, and to see the son of the ill-fated Wickenham standing there threadbare, daring the wrath of Greywalls for the sake of his impoverished guardian, moved unfamiliar mists across her eyes. She looked past him at the tangled garden where weeds were and Shaddy was not, and compassion shone through for a moment when the mists cleared.

'Don't know what Master Jeffries will think on 'un,'

she mused, 'But then, need Master Jeffries be told?' She was in charge, and Jeffries, when in residence, rarely came into the kitchen garden. 'If 'ee do keep well away from the house, and not come at all when Miss James do be here,' Clements said, 'and do work proper under Shaddy …'

The conditions seemed endless, but eventually it was agreed – that if he became an invisible boy, and came not at all while Hannah was there, he might earn up to fourpence an hour. The deal was then pledged with a corner of pasty, which Shaddy Bunt noted with the gastric juices of envy as he peered from his retreat in the shrubbery.

Predictably, Daddy Joseph said no. The stigma of a son of his being employed by the grey house could not be sustained. Phoebe disagreed and prevailed. '*What* son of yours?' she asked bluntly in private. All Crigga knew it not to be true, and for years she had warned him that Brendin must be lost to the grey house. It was better like this, when all fisherfolk were taking desperate means, than in less understandable circumstances later. 'Either tes this, or what I did say for the boat,' she said finally, 'Ent possible for 'ee to go on like this, Joe Pendenna.' At last, he wavered and bent. Stretched on the rack of events, each torturing turn was becoming too much for him. Silently he went down to the quay and, in the dappled waters of evening, sought to re-enact the placidity of yesteryears – as old men will in the titillating flames of a fire.

Brendin lay awake that night, agog at the day's events and the new dimension that had entered his life. He longed to be able to talk of his adventure with the evangelist and ask questions about the intriguing Wickenham, but with instinctive wisdom he refrained – recoiling from memories of similar inquisitiveness in the past.

'Old wives' tales, children's notions,' Phoebe would say when he mentioned the hauntings. 'Do 'ee get such nonsense out of your head.' And Joe would sit grey-faced and aloof.

'Who was Sara,' Brendin asked Phoebe once.

'My dear life, boy, there do be Sara's a-plenty,' she had replied shortly. 'They'm in the graveyard and out of it. Your own mam was a Sara. Now do 'ee hush, boy.' And that was all she would say.

Lying there gazing through the open door at a glint of moonlight illuminating the old sea chest in the kitchen corner, he peopled his mind with visions. Tonight, there was little wind, but the tide rode high and he could hear the glug of waves chopping away at the cliff base, waves that had swept on from the cove, the cove that was so strongly in his thoughts in those moments that he felt an overwhelming yearning to leave the cottage and go there.

'Sara's a-plenty, in the graveyard and out of it ...' Phoebe's phrase throbbed in his consciousness till, as he slept, mystic Sara was everywhere – thronging the room, murmuring to the lilt of the tide, rising from the long-smoothed grave, and reaching out to a voiceless wraith whose arms she could never meet...

Brendin took avidly to the work at the grey house. Each day – after school or in hours during the weekends – he would slip round to the side-door beloved of Hannah and toil at the tasks of weeding or cutting hedges. Shaddy, resentful at first, soon recognised the value of a young pair of hands which enabled him to enact a foreman's role from a snug in the shrubbery. Yet he avoided Brendin, his thin coating of conscience susceptible to the boy's likeness to the father he supposed he had drowned.

'Remember this boy,' he said thickly one evening,

brandy-breathed from the drowning of memories, 'I ent never done no harm to anyone. Tes lies. Tes all lies what they tell 'ee.'

'Tell me what?' Brendin asked.

'Nothin'. I did say nothin'. Tes lies.'

Puzzled, Brendin braved Clements and asked what he meant. Reticent at first, she explained that once, long ago, a man had been trapped by the tide and Shaddy could have warned him. 'But,' she admonished, 'you ent here to gossip, young man. Do 'ee get along with the work and leave Shaddy alone.'

'Ess, missus.' But again, he left with his curiosity unresolved.

The pattern continued without incident until July, when, for Brendin, irretrievable disaster suddenly struck. To her bitter self-recrimination it was Clements herself, lulled into complacency, who set the fuse. She had noticed a bad patch of weeds in the drive. Hannah was due that day, Shaddy had set out for the station, and Brendin was about to depart till the summer's end, when she halted him. Jeffries would arrive soon and Shaddy could not be relied on.

'Quick boy,' she told him, 'do 'ee tidy this up before 'ee go.'

But Brendin was not quick enough. The train was early and, before he could gather his tools, the jingle was halting beside him. He looked up in the hope of smiling a greeting to Hannah, then gasped as he met the bristling gaze of an outraged Jeffries.

For a second the tableau held, the prologue to a drama in the summer sunshine – Jeffries glaring with an unbelieving awe at the unmistakable image of Wickenham, come into his very fastness to fan into life the smouldering tragedy of the past.

He swung to the unhappy Clements, 'What is the

meaning of this? What is the boy doing here? Eh?'

Even then she contrived to appear unperturbed. 'He be helping with the weeding sir, that be all.'

'All? *All*? *This* boy, in *my* garden? Have you taken leave of your wits, woman?' He levered himself from the jingle, and to Hannah, 'Get you inside, miss, and wait till I come.' Hannah, with one scared, bewildered look at Brendin, complied. Shaddy led the jingle hastily away.

'The boy,' Clements said gallantly, 'ent doing no harm.'

'No harm, ma'am? No harm, is it? You have eyes that see? Eh? You have studied the boy?'

'I do see, sir. All that there be to see. He be but weeding for a penny or two.'

Jeffries turned on Brendin. 'Then take a penny or two.' He thrust a hand in his pocket and threw down a handful of silver and copper. 'Now be off, boy. Go. Go! And don't you ever – and by God, I mean never – ever come near to this house again.' He swung back to Clements. 'There is more to be said, ma'am.'

Brendin, shocked and dazed by the onslaught, found in the denigration a standpoint for courage and pride. White-lipped he said, 'Ent no proper talk for a gentleman, and you'll be sorry for 'un. I can only be what I be.' He turned with an inbred dignity that made Jeffries wince and, leaving the coins on the ground, went down the drive and out of the gate.

Once on the headland, a choking lump grew in his throat. He knew he was somehow wrong for the Crigga folk but had consoled himself with the thought that at least he had been accepted on the periphery of Greywalls. Now he felt rejected by everyone. There was no need to tell Phoebe and Joe what had happened, for they knew he was barred from the holidays. He made his way to the hollow, with little hope that Hannah would be able to come – or would want to after his humiliation at the house and sat there miserably staring at the unforgiving sea.

But Hannah did come, glancing carefully round, tender with sympathy, 'Only a moment,' she whispered, 'or they will miss me.'

'I be sorry, Hannah.'

'Oh, Brendin.' Snuggling by the ridge of the hollow she searched his face anxiously and held his hand. 'It is me who is sorry. What a shame Uncle Jeffries had to come today. Everything would have been so lovely. And he treated you dreadfully.'

'Because I be from the village, I suppose.'

'But you're different,' she said, and he grimaced.

'That be why,' he murmured with insight, 'Nobody wants me.'

'I do, silly. But what *were* you doing at Greywalls?'

He told the story, 'A shilling or two for Daddy Joseph. But it be finished now.'

'Poor dear Brendin, it isn't fair.' She squeezed the hand she still held and he looked up into wide grey eyes – regarding him from a depth he had not known before. Surely, when rock flowed in primal liquidity, this hollow was fashioned as a sanctuary for yearning hearts: for Hannah and Brendin, Sara and Philip, John Michal and Ruth – bearing only the echoed sighing of generations that had gone before.

'I must go,' she murmured, 'And don't be upset. I will see you tomorrow.' She lifted before him till he could feel the brush of her hair against his forehead, paused – half frightened – then sought his lips. It was a quick, shy kiss. 'Juliet was only fourteen,' she said, 'and we're *nearly* fourteen.'

'Who be – Who is Juliet?' he asked.

Hannah smiled. 'They were lovers – Romeo and

would say no more and, since echoes of stertorous slumber now came from the parlour, he was forced to leave the matter there. But he was deeply pensive as he threaded his way back. Sam, always cryptic towards him, had been positive this time. Unless the brandy had stirred hallucinations, the old man had a potent recollection from the past.

He was rounding the outer wall of the churchyard, when he recognised the evangelist's van with Captain Soames standing beside it. They looked at each other – Brendin expectantly, Soames with a puzzled glance of semi-recognition. Brendin halted.

'I should know you,' said Soames, 'for I never forget a face. Wait a minute – such a familiar face!'

'It is a few years since I met you, sir. Brendin Pendenna from Crigga.' He offered his hand, and Soames clasped it.

'Pendenna? Pendenna. Of course. The boy, now a man – and a most presentable young man, just like… Oh, dear, I do believe I'm muddling you up.'

'Muddling me with?'

'Somebody I once knew.' He changed the subject, 'You've a fine suit of clothes, young man.'

'I had a slight change of fortune, sir. I work now.'

'Ah.' He regarded him closely. 'By the change in attire, young man, anyone could see the resemblance to … but that's impossible,' the evangelist stammered.

'Resemblance?'

'To … to a gentleman – but no matter. Come inside, sir, and give me an account of yourself. Do.'

Brendin looked at the blackening sky. 'It can't be for long, sir. There's a storm coming up and the tide will be over the bridge.'

'Ah, yes.' Soames followed an upward glance to see ebony wisps attaching themselves from the main scurries of cloud, and thunder cracked from the west. 'Just a moment, then. You have often been in my thoughts.'

'I've looked for you once or twice,' Brendin told him. 'You do not come every year?'

'Oh no my boy, no. I have many circuits. But wherever we travel, we all seek the same path at last.'

'Do you preach?'

'I run a mission in London, where the distressed and lonely can come …' Brendin listened keenly as Soames outlined his work among the derelict and needy, the rescuing and rehabilitation of those who, in the eyes of the everyday world, were worth nothing. 'Not a text down their throats like a cup of tea,' he said, 'but a human application of the good Lord's teaching – making them feel that at last they belong.'

'Belonging – yes,' Brendin said wistfully, 'I understand that.'

Soames put a friendly hand on the boy's shoulder. 'You belong, Brendin,' he coughed, 'You still like to read?'

'Yes, sir. I earn a little now and I have a tutor – once a week in Truro. He does it for the love of it and so he is very cheap. I have learned about the Greek and the Roman heroes, how to write in a fine hand – all sorts of things …'

'An education!'

'Of sorts – but I really wish I could learn who I really am.'

The conversation was drowned out by a trundle of thunder that growled from the further wastes of the ocean and relapsed with a staccato crack against the hills inland. 'You'd better hurry my boy,' Soames urged. And slipping a card into Brendin's pocket: 'Should you ever need anything – anything at all – you will find me here.'

Brendin thanked him and set off for Crigga with an

impending sense of occasion – not entirely due to the ominous loom of the weather. Old Sam's remarks were not easily forgettable, and Soames had also given him cause to wonder, for surely, he too had noticed a resemblance – but to whom?

'Grey house! Grey house!' a bunch of young Pascoes yelled at him as he came to the road – putting a seal on his sense of otherness. The wind was gusting to gale force now, and clouds hovered like jet mountains above and around the liquid valley of the bay.

Over the plank bridge the tide was already at ankle lap, rising, and darkness was coming down early. The storm moaned and above it the groan of the battling column mourned in human accompaniment as folk strove to gain foothold on and over the bridge. Brendin and others, waist high in the swirling water each side of the flimsy timbers, urged and helped them across, till the tide began flooding laterally over the sand, leaving unhappy remnants struggling to cross from the Pennan shore. Directly into the storm the main body pushed on and over the Pennan headland to the dunes leading to Crigga.

'Christ, save any craft on a lee shore tonight,' panted a fisherman and, as if to mark his fear, a distress rocket flew up suddenly to light the skies above Crigga Bay. Men ran against the gust, Brendin among them, as a second rocket went up. Clothes streaming and throats dry they skirted the old harbour, pushed up and onto the headland.

On the cliffs groups of watchers – helpless in the face of the wind and the raging waves – were peering into the dusk. The stricken boat could be dimly seen, masts gone, and her beam end, fast disappearing into the seething sea. She had driven clean onto the Reaper Rocks – the merciless teeth a mile north of the headland point, too far out for a breeches buoy, too far gone to be reached in time by lifeboat or other craft.

'Tes, the old Katie,' someone was saying. 'God save their souls.'

Brendin felt a long shiver grip him. So, Davey was gone. Dear honest Davey who had still called him Boyo, who had shared his lunch, who had spun yarns about far-off places and dragons, and was one of the few friends he had ever known. He strayed sadly away from the main body of sight seers towards the top of the cove, turned his head from the wind, and unashamedly sobbed and challenged God.

Now, entranced, he turned his eyes to the cave – fixed, drawn like a pin into a magnetic field. Below, was a chaos of shuddering rock pounded by a demented sea, but from it rose forces impervious to physical stress, and from them an invisible power that entered and gripped him. For a chilling moment it was as though he became the power itself, not Brendin. Then another voice – wavered clear from the wind. It came low, sweetly plaintive, like a siren he had learned about – wheedling lost souls. It projected a name – not 'Sara, Sara!' recalled from the past, but, 'Brendin! Brendin!'

The call came again, insistently, appealingly, and at last, he slowly looked round from the brink. A figure stood poised on the upper slope, dimly familiar, draped in a shimmering white cape and hat. Once more it pleaded, entreating, arms outstretched: 'Brendin, Brendin, it's Hannah. Don't you remember me?'

'Hannah?' came an echo borne on the wind. He paused for a long while as though torn between conflicting enticements.

'Brendin!' she cried again.

And at length, like a puppet urged against the pull of elastic, he began inching towards her up the slope. With eager care she put out a hand to aid him, eyes anxiously searching his face.

'Hannah, Hannah,' he seemed to mouth vaguely.

She closed her eyes, and when she opened them, Brendin looked at her in wonder, thankfully and with growing relief.

Of all the reunions she had conjured during the bleak years of separation, Hannah had never imagined a reunion like this. She had only just arrived from the afternoon train when the distress rockets flared, and she had hurried in her sou'wester to join the watchers on the cliffs. She had searched vainly for Brendin among the jostling crowd, until catching sight of a young man detached from the others, straying towards the rim of the never-forgotten cove. That it must be Brendin she was sure, for there was something unmistakable about the bearing and the look of him, and she had made her way to the hollow – only to watch in helpless fear as he swayed on the brink of the precipice. Now she clung to him, closely, silently, relieved but still trembling, but Brendin, though conscious of the pull of the cove, seemed unaware of the danger. Her one aim, in the bliss of their renewed togetherness, was to coax him away from the place that seemed to have such a mesmeric effect on him.

'Come away into the hollow,' she urged. But he still faintly registered, his eyes questing towards the drop.

'It is a strange spot,' he murmured,' as in a semi-dream. 'They did not believe me, Hannah,' but twice I've sensed a ghost – once in the cove, and once in the cave beyond. And tonight ...' He shook his head in a daze.

'You saw something tonight?' Chill tremors crept up her spine.

'No,' he said absently, 'But if you had not come... I am drawn. I am always drawn.'

'Brendin – my love, you must try to resist.'

'Yes'... But the word was without conviction. Then:

'No, Hannah, I can't. Sooner or later, I shall have to *know*.'

'Sooner or later. Please come away – now. *Please*.'

This time he allowed himself to be tugged away, but on the rim of the hollow he stopped. 'Hannah,' have you heard of a poet called Wickenham?'

'Well, yes,' she answered reluctantly, 'I have seen some of his verse. And Clements told me that he was once a guest at Greywalls. Why?'

The gale whistled with renewed venom, whipping the words from his lips.

'Did you know he was trapped in the cove?'

'No,' she whispered, and was pierced by creeping, unexplained anxiety. Her voice quivered to a higher octave. 'Brendin, *dear* Brendin – it has been *years*. I have come back to you. Don't talk about this.'

She looked very lovely there, white faced, her eyes bright in the darkness, her whole attitude plaintive. 'Please, Brendin. *Please*.'

His heart leapt at the beauty and loyalty of her, unbelievably true to a love for him over seemingly hopeless years. He led her into the calm of the hollow and they kissed as the rain poured down, deluge and hurricane forgotten in the magic of whispered words.

'They thought I would forget … I thought I had died when they took me away … but I never stopped thinking of you and loving you … and now I am back … and whatever happens we shall be together forever …'

'Where have you been all this time, my darling Hannah?'

'Oh, learning to be a lady.'

'There's no need for *that*.' With a gentle finger he traced the droplets of rain across the curve of her brow, 'You could have written to me.'

'I thought of it, but it was terrible at first. They

watched me always. Then I thought it might make things worse for you, and afterwards I wondered if you still felt the same.'

'I was dead, too,' he said, 'It was only with you that I ever belonged.'

'It's true,' she breathed happily, 'I know it's true. All I wanted to do when I got here was come straight out and find you. They thought it was over – but it's only just begun!'

Her arms stole round him, and words became puny things. The kiss was a continuation of the shy giving so many years ago, absorbing the present and embracing a far future.

'Say you love me,' she said.

'Hannah – I love you.'

'She kissed him again.'

'And you will never leave me?'

'I will *never* leave you.'

REVELATION

His thoughts were a strange tangle as he bid Hannah goodnight and made for the Pendenna cottage: Sam Curnow, Soames, the storm, poor Davey, the weird, fleeting sensation by the cove and, pervading all, the timely, miraculous return of his dearest love, Hannah. It was late when he reached the little dwelling he had always known as home.

Daddy Joseph looked at Brendin quizzically, 'Where have 'ee been, boy? Down by the tide? I expected 'ee two or three hours since.'

'It was a hard task from Pennan,' Brendin said briefly,' and I've been watching the wreck.' Then, with the need for honesty, 'I saw Hannah – the girl from the grey house.'

'Ah, so *she* do be back, then?'

'Yes, she is back, Daddy Joe.'

For a moment, Pendenna's eyes flashed, and their glances met in a sharp understanding of conflict. Then the ageing fisherman relaxed. 'Do 'ee take care, now. The troubles ent over yet,' and he retired up the narrow stairs to his bed.

Brendin lingered to savour the humble peace of the kitchen. Phoebe had left a pasty on the table, and the fire still stuttered a dispassionate welcome. He sat in the chimney corner, drowsily trying to unravel the ciphers in the flickering flames. So much had happened in so little time, superimposed on the already chaotic pattern of memories, that from mingled fatigue and wonder, it seemed as though a different person altogether was experiencing them.

The light coaxed dull reflection from the battered sea-chest in the opposite corner, in which reposed relics of

Pendenna's more orthodox days. Above it, the little window, un-curtained, clipped a square pattern from the outer dark. For a long while Brendin kept his gaze in the window, as if mesmerised, his eyes vainly trying to probe the tunnel of light that led from it to the fringing sea.

Gradually, his gaze became fixed on the old sea-chest which relapsed like an ancient monument to the past in the further corner. For years, he had studied the relic vaguely, with no heed for the trifles that might be stored within. Now he went to it with sudden purpose. It lay in a shaft of moonlight, in its drab framework of leather and wood. He felt urged towards it and looked around carefully to ensure that none watched – save, perhaps, some spectre from the past. No visible eyes challenged him, and Brendin bent to the chest.

The huge padlock was closed and stiff. The key had been lost long since and, with a creak, the shaft yielded to the strength of his hand and the lid lay defenceless against his leverage. He gripped patiently, easing around the rim and the chest came slowly open.

Inside, illumined by the moonlight, lay the unconsidered flotsam of many nautical years: an ancient quadrant, a sailor's head on an ornamental rope, the brass plate of a ship, lanyards, an ensign or two, a battered old compass – worn and stained artefacts from a past once worshipped, now only invoked by the incense of mustiness. Brendin turned them over with a murmur of sympathy and was about to readjust them and close the lid when he saw the book.

It was a slim, leather-bound volume mildewed with the years and, by its worn appearance, obviously well used before that. He picked it up and wondered, surprised at such a find in the Pendenna cottage, where books were hardly known to exist. The gilt lettering on the cover was still faintly visible: *The Wickenham Book of Verse.*

Wickenham. Dear God! The poet they say was drowned in the cove. The mysterious visitor to the grey house, whom no-one knew and would never answer questions about. A weird, griping tremble rippled over him and he fought with a sudden lump in his throat. Trancelike he opened the book, scanning the middle pages. Many of the verses were underlined, and he muttered as he traced out a few of them. '*As in a dream beyond a darkening room… Voices within my voice… Ageless through age-long years… Make me not walk alone …*'

Tremulously, hardly believing, he turned to the flyleaf. Without warning, a cloud sped and engulfed the moon. He waited in silence till the light filtered again in reluctant patches from the window – then looked once more at the book. The inscription, though faded, burned out from the page: '*Sara Michal, 1882.*'

Barely conscious of what he was doing, Brendin shut the book, slipped it in his pocket and closed the lid of the chest, aware of a new vitally revealing dimension. A fisher-girl in this bookless dwelling, owning, and marking with such care, a volume of Wickenham's verse? Which Sara? He recalled Phoebe's dismissive statement, 'There do be Saras a-plenty, in the graveyard and out of it. Your own mam was a Sara ...' And it was 'Sara… Sara…' that had echoed from the cove and the cave.

The implications were clear. So many things were now coming together, too many and too quickly for his shocked and exhausted state. He went wearily to the bedroom and lay just as he was, to fall into dream-haunted sleep – peopled with visions and long-standing memories: 'Grey house! Grey house!... Sara! Sara!' Then came Soames mouthing 'Wickenham,' and Sam chuckling, 'That bastard from Lunnon,' and a witch-like figure, remote from his infancy, croaking, 'Begone little bastard, or I won't answer for 'ee …'

Brendin, after a night of tangled rest, was up long before Daddy Joe, roaming the cliffs waiting the appearance of Hannah, and still trying to admit the evidence of yesterday into his reluctant mind. For if admissible, the whole tenor of his life was changed. He yearned now for the tender understanding of Hannah. They had grown so close, and he could not conceive any future existence without her, his one durable link with the wider horizons he had always instinctively sought.

At dawn the beaches were already thronged with sightseers, salvage hunters and officials marshalling the timbers and other remnants drifting ashore from the luckless Katie. These, if not born surreptitiously away, would be auctioned in lots – a shoddy end for a once proud little schooner. 'There are jinxes, boyo,' Davey had once told him, and they had callously struck, down from the howling heavens and up from the indifferent sea.

Hannah came to him on the sands. She, too, had been up early and glimpsed him from the library window. 'Brendin!' she called. As she approached, she was surprised, in the light of day, to see a gentleman standing before her – not only in bearing, but in his manner of dress, for it had been dark, and he had been drenched and dishevelled the night before, giving him an excuse to put on his best suit of clothes.

'But what …?'

'As you see, I have had a little good fortune since our parting – an education and a modest income. My dearest Hannah, I have so much to tell you.'

They moved away from the beach and towards the headland, heedless of curious glances, eyes only for each other in the new-found contentment of reunion. Today they bypassed the hollow and strolled down to the old harbour, where there was rugged peace under the cloud-blown sky. Once there, Hannah scanned his face closely, 'You look tired,' my love.'

'It has been a strange night.' He took her hand as they sat on a great granite boulder in the lee of the cliff. 'I have something else to tell you.'

'And I have something to show *you*.' She looked enquiringly up at him. 'But you tell me first.'

It was difficult to begin with, raising again the subject of the cove, but once he had started, and was sure of her sympathy, the whole story came out: of his bewildered childhood, the never answered questions, the complete silence regarding any mention of his mother, the unresolved feeling of non-belonging, the nocturnal return to the cove, and finally – the discovery of the old book in the sea-chest.

'This,' he said, showing it to her, 'published by Jeffries. There is the link with the grey house.'

'And *this*,' and Hannah drew another volume from the handbag she carried. The book was newer, larger, and she read: 'The Collected Poems of Philip Wickenham. I wondered about him last night,' she explained, 'and I searched for him in the library. There is nothing of him on the shelves or in the catalogues, but this one was hidden under a pile of discards in the corner. It's a different publisher – from America. And, oh, Brendin …' She looked at him, wide-eyed, with a mixture of fear and disbelief, then buried her face on his shoulder and held him close.

For a while he soothed her. 'What is it?'

Drawing away, she held out the book. He took it, puzzled. The same poems, a few new ones, nothing especially marked, a glowing tribute to the acclaimed poet and, opposite this, a full-face photograph of the author. A shock wave trembled through Brendin. The face was older, but the person portrayed was *himself*, the features in the photograph – the same! And there was a further mystery: Wickenham's biography gave the date of his birth – but *not* his death. What is more, the volume was dated *after* the early encounters in the cove!

There was no need for words, even if those moments could have managed to frame them. In the face of such evidence the implication was inescapable. Everything was beginning to come together to solve the riddle of years.

Slowly, Brendin disengaged and stood up. 'I will come back soon, darling. I must see Daddy Joe at once.'

It was still early. Phoebe had just arrived to attend to the morning chores when Brendin appeared. She turned in surprise, 'Ah, there you be, boy. I were wondering.'

'Where's Daddy Joseph?' As if in answer, he heard Pendenna coming downstairs. 'Phoebe,' he said, 'Will you go for a while? I must talk to Daddy Joe.'

'Dear souls,' Phoebe complained, 'you can talk to 'un, then. Ent no call for me to go, you.'

'This time, yes.' He spoke with a sudden edge of authority. 'Phoebe, I want to talk to Daddy Joe – alone.'

She looked at his face, whitely determined and, with a grumbling, 'My dear heart, don't know where 'ee be to,' flung down the cloth she was using and shuffled through the door.

'What be this, boy?' Daddy Joe asked.

For answer Brendin took Wickenham's book from his pocket and held it up before Joe. Pendenna's eyes went blank for a moment, then with sudden flame shot to the book, the sea chest, and with anger to Brendin.

'Where did 'ee get that then, boy?'

'You know where I got it from.'

'You ent got no right ...'

Brendin's head shook and he was deathly tense. 'I've got every right. Daddy Joe, why didn't you tell me? What have I to do with Sara Michal and Philip Wickenham?'

Pendenna, his face drawn, was silent.

'For God's sake, speak,' Brendin urged, 'tell me. In Christ's name, who am I?'

Daddy Joe stood there, head bent, bowed with the intolerable burden of a secret carried for twenty distressful years. Deflated, he sank into a chair. 'Ess,' he said wearily, 'ess boy, I should have told 'ee. I should have told 'ee, be 'ee come up to twenty-one.'

'They're my father and mother?'

Joe found the words hard to say. Then at last, 'Ess, boy, ess, they do be.'

'Then what am I doing here?'

Joe Pendenna sighed. 'Sit 'ee down, boy, sit 'ee down.' The confession made, he haltingly revealed the whole story – as far as he knew, how the poet was believed dead, and that the boy's mother had died in childbirth soon afterwards.

Brendin looked with wonder and pity at the ageing man who had selflessly taken on and fulfilled such a demanding promise. 'And all these years you've said nothing and looked after me?'

'I did love the maid, dearly,' Pendenna murmured.

'And Wickenham – my father, he did much wrong, didn't he?'

'Ent for me to speak ill of the dead.'

'But he did? And was sorry for it? Not only here – What of his wife in London?'

Daddy Joe shook his head sadly, 'Ess,' he conceded, 'I suppose he did much wrong – but he do be punished.'

'How – punished?'

'Never found 'un. Ent in holy ground. Mebbe the fish

had 'un. Ent that punishment enough?'

Brendin shuddered at the image, and flooding his mind once more came the desperate cry, re-echoing from a trap in the rocky walls of the cave.

'Ent in holy ground,' Pendenna repeated.

'Dear Lord,' Brendin sighed, 'and my mother – Sara?'

Pendenna paused. 'She be in the churchyard,' and dripping beads of sweat, passed a handkerchief across his brow. 'Now tes done. You be grey house, boy, and ent no-one here will ever stand in your way.'

Brendin sat motionless for a while. Then he rose and touched Joe's shoulder as he turned to go. He was deeply moved, for it had been the first gesture of companionship between them when Pendenna reached up and gripped his hand. Brendin nodded in response and said, 'I shall go to the churchyard now.'

THE GOSSOMER CHAIN

'You be the grey house, boy.' The words echoed in Brendin's ears as he walked slowly in bewilderment from the cottage. Everything now should be falling precisely into place, but in some respects the answer was still frustratingly incomplete. Like a torch in a darkened room, the beam of Pendenna's blunt, unembroidered revelation had illumined the centre – leaving remoter corners more shrouded than before.

His thoughts jostled with each other, playing with jigsaws, but when he reached the churchyard and knelt before his mother's grave, a transient peace descended. It was as though his soul was filled with poetry unborn, but unable to capture it, he whispered a short prayer.

As he left the churchyard and struck out across the headland, he reflected on the unforgiving enmity of Jeffries – encompassing two bitter generations, which seemed strangely out of proportion to the wrong committed. Perhaps there was a professional argument – due to Wickenham seeking another publisher. The later edition had not been given space in Jeffries' library but had been obscured by a pile of unwanted books yet to be sorted out.

There were still so many unanswered questions – about Sara and the poet, on whom Joe was reluctant to dwell – even about his own Hannah. And permeating all, the voice trapped in the cave, which he now supposed was his father's. All this affected him constantly, not with the grim forcefulness of the cove, but like an enveloping mist, an intangible gossamer chain that constantly bound him. What further secrets lay undisclosed, and what more must he do to be free from it all?

Hannah was waiting on the headland, reading

Wickenham's verse in the sunshine, and looked up with a questioning glance.

'It is so,' Brendin said, 'Daddy Joseph has told me. I am what the old woman described.' He sat down beside her. 'Sara Michal was my mother. She died when I was born. After my father was thought drowned, poor Daddy Joe took her in and adopted me.' He bowed his head. 'God, not a word over all these years.'

'Brendin, my dear – I know what this must be for you.'

'If only I'd known, it might have been different.'

'No.' She felt for his hand, 'It wasn't your fault. There's nothing you could have done. Do not reproach yourself.'

'I could have been kinder to Joe.'

'But you told me – you tried.'

Listlessly he rose and walked to the tide rim, flinging a stone in the water, watching pensively as the gulls rose from the sound in a feathered arc.

After a while Hannah joined him. She hesitated. 'And your father *was* – really *was* Wickenham?'

He turned to her, 'Yes. I'm sorry, my love, I'm in a terrible muddle – but at least I know now where I belong.'

'You belong to me,' she said quietly, 'We belong together, and we will face things together. Nothing can alter that.'

He smiled one of his rare smiles, took her face in his hands and whispered, 'Bless you for coming back.'

'And bless you for being here. Whoever you are, whatever happens, I shall never leave you again.'

They strolled along hand in hand, silently. From the waiting years, a fleeting contentment had at last emerged. It was pure, unselfish love – a wordless ecstasy coaxed from the touch of eternal things. Surely Wickenham's shade from a sad mind must have wandered there in the time-cancelled tracks of his Sara – wondering at the imprints of a new generation.

In a while Hannah stopped, tracing with raptured eyes the hillocks of sand and the long line of breakers that stretched like a hem of foam from headland to headland. 'It is beautiful,' she sighed, 'Wickenham must have loved it. Well, I know that he did. I read in the book this morning: *As tide-rims mark the equidistant shore ...*'

'*As parallels flow on and never meet ...*' Brendin quoted immediately, and she glanced at him in surprise. 'Why, Brendin, you know it.'

'It was one of the quotes underlined by Sara,' he told her, 'It isn't so strange.' Yet when she spoke his whole thoughts had been a jumble of poetry. He could not get it out of his head, and had she asked, could have quoted more of the poem –

Our lines are drawn apart for ever more –
Diverge-less, unrelenting, incomplete.
Yet who can doubt, if we could only see
In sanctified dimensions of a finer kind
We are not ruled by quaint geometry,
But blend in the true aspects of the mind ...

It was strange, but he said nothing for a while, then: 'I understood he was a romantic, but this is clearly metaphysical, don't you think – or a blending of both?'

'That's very profound,' she laughed, 'How do you know all that?'

'My darling Hannah, you forget – I had a good tutor – cheap, but very good.'

'Forgive me, of course, my love.' Hannah studied him. 'Perhaps you will be a poet. But what will you do now? What shall *we* do?'

'I don't know,' he said, 'I must try and find out about myself and do the right thing.'

'We will marry,' she said positively, 'Nothing can stop us now.'

He smiled at her eagerness. 'My love, I am nothing. I have very little. I have my education, I know – and a little money.'

'It doesn't matter. You are everything – the son of a famous father – and I shall have money when I come of age.'

'I could not take your money – whatever I decide to do. Besides, you are not quite of age yet and they still have control of you.'

She shook her head impulsively. 'Then we'll run away.'

'No,' he countered, 'we will not run away. There's been enough running away and deceitfulness. We will face up to whatever there is, do what is right. Otherwise, there will never be peace. It will be the same miserable story all over again.'

'Oh, Brendin,' she laughed, 'you're a funny boy. I love you dearly, but sometimes I think I don't know you at all.'

'Well, I don't know myself, do I? Sometimes I seem to be two people. You must bear with me, my dearest.'

She took his arm as they strolled slowly.

'It *is* funny, isn't it? We played together for years, and there were all those long separations. But we never doubted each other.'

'Or questioned each other,' he added, 'To me you were just the little girl from the grey house, and that was enough. I knew very little about you.'

She grimaced. 'I'm ordinary, not mysterious like you. Ordinary little Hannah James.'

'No, Hannah. But your people?'

'Oh, father died last year, and …'

'Hannah, I'm sorry …'

'Oh, that's alright. Daddy was always away on business.'

'Has your mother been to Crigga?'

'No. Poor Mummy can't travel. But Uncle Jeffs has always been very good to us – although he's ever so strict, of course.'

'Is he at the grey house – Greywalls – now?'

'No – thank goodness. He'd have a fit if he saw us. We must be very careful.' She pouted ruefully. 'If you won't run away ...'

He gripped her hand. 'I love you, Hannah, but I must do this my way.'

'And what *is* your way?'

He cringed from upsetting her trust. 'I must get used to who and what I am – then speak to Jeffries and your mother. If they will not agree, then we must take it from there.'

She watched him intently. 'Brendin, please let it be soon – because always something happens to keep us apart. Please, please don't let it happen again.'

The sun dipped to a sliver of red across the grim Crigga headland, and suddenly there came the eldritch scream, the premonitory lament of the crake.

Like water on powder, darkness dissolves the optimism of the day. Brendin sensed that his trials were held in suspension under the Crigga sun, but now the colour was fading with the returning night, the atmosphere of depression visible. Hannah sensed it too, tightening her grip on his arm. 'We must go now, it's as if I'm seeing Crigga for the very first time – like a dark, haunted island ...'

'Yes, we will go.' He stifled his own unease.

It was as though there were two Criggas: Crigga of beauty he loved, and the other that stole insidiously from the cove. If the latter could – somehow – be resolved, there could be nothing but content.

They moved forward, the dark mass of headland seeming to follow them like a stalking animal, its profile menacing against the sea and sky. Despite this, Brendin felt a surge of pity for the remembered voice that had been trapped in the cave below, still playing out an unfathomable living death in the gloom. But why?

The captivating influence brought deep unease. Was his father's wraith sorry for the life he had bequeathed the son he was never to meet?

He took Hannah's hand, 'You had better go home, or Clements will be worrying.'

She hesitated with growing foreboding, with the prophetic sense that her happiness could not last. She knew that he feared the same. Both arms wrapped round one of his, 'I can't bear to leave you. Let me walk with you – just a few steps.'

'No. You must go now, little Hannah.' He turned towards the hollow.

'Well – What are you going to do?'

'Nothing. Just stay here for a while, that's all.'

'You're not ...' she trembled, 'You're not going down to the cove?'

'No. Now go, my love. I shall see you tomorrow.'

'But Brendin ...'

He knew she had not gone. He glimpsed her, wide-eyed, disappearing like a bird into a cloud and, faintly through the mist enveloping his senses, came her despairing cry: 'Brendin!' Then all aspects faded, and he was on the headland path again – Hannah clinging to him.

'The cove – it's the cove!' she cried, 'You could have been drowned. It will take you away from me. Oh, Brendin, can't you see? We must go away.'

By shuddering degrees, some confidence returned. He

took her hand and led her back to the grey house. 'Dear God, Hannah,' he murmured, 'I love you more than my life – and against all the powers on earth. Now go indoors, my love.' He touched her shoulder gently. 'You were right. We must go away. I shall go to London to see your family tomorrow.'

'Then I shall come with you.'

He shook his head. 'This is something I must tackle myself. And once it is over ...' He kissed her, 'We shall be together for always. Come to the station with me early tomorrow.'

But as he spoke, he felt mocked by the sneer of fate.

Pendenna, sitting by the fireside, glanced up expectantly as Brendin came in. 'You be tired, boy.'

'I've been with Hannah,' he spat it out, 'I'm thinking of marrying her.'

But Joe was resigned, 'Ess, boy.'

'I'm going to London tomorrow to see her family.'

'Be 'ee, boy?'

'And we shall go away somewhere.'

'Ess, boy? How do 'ee think to get on?'

'I shall find a job – as a tutor, perhaps – teaching reading and writing. I have some education. You'll be alright with the boat. Business is good now.'

'Ent no call to fret about me.'

'Yes. I'll come and see you when we're settled and ...'

'Ent no call.'

'Oh, but there is. Well, goodnight, Daddy Joe.'

Pendenna stood up and raised an arresting hand. 'Do 'ee hold a moment, boy.'

'Yes, Daddy Joe?'

'Ent the only one boy. I've a mind now to wed Phoebe – proper like.'

Brendin clasped him strongly by the hand. 'I'm so glad for you both – you deserve to be happy, Daddy Joe.'

Daddy Joe sank back in his chair – to dream of unlimited pasties and a mountain of feminine flesh, while Brendin went to his room hoping for rest.

He had not mentioned his real reason for leaving Crigga – the sinister attraction to the cove, for Pendenna had already discounted such stories and had no stomach for their resurrection. But for Brendin, the lure of the cove was terrible and real. If only for Hannah's sake, much as he loved Crigga, the only solution was to get away from the whole, possessive arena. Yet he was still filled with haunting concern for the unhappy Wickenham's supposed shade, But Hannah must always come first …

On the verges of sleep, strangely prophetic echoes of Wickenham's verse pursued him: *As in a dream beyond a darkening room … Voices within my voice …* One voice was the voice of Hannah, breathing, 'We shall be together for always …'

She met him in the morning, and they walked slowly to the station. It was an emotive hour, and little was said. It was the first time Brendin had left Crigga and, when he held her in parting, there was the faintest quiver of foreboding – as though an unseen power felt compassion for their aching goodbye.

'I shall be back soon, my love,' he assured her, 'Surely they will be reasonable, and then …' The sudden shriek of a whistle swept his last words.

'Goodbye, darling Brendin. I shall be waiting.' The train began moving. 'I love you!' she called.

He strained from a carriage window until, on the distant platform, Hannah was a remote figure waving a handkerchief and, in an eddy of smoke and steam, the train puffed around the bend, and she was gone.

'Goodbye – dear Hannah,' he echoed.

CONFRONTATION

He arrived. His ears rang from the clatter of traffic – where omnibuses and carts jostled for space. The city air was offensive after the pure ocean breathings of Crigga, and the endless hurrying of the populace seemed to serve only the purpose of conveying them into a continuous circle back to where they began. But he suffered it gladly for his momentous task.

Hannah had drawn a rough map and given him both Jeffries' and her family's addresses and, at her persuasion that Jeffries was always the influential voice, he decided to go there first. The sooner the confrontation was over, the better.

Brendin, dressed in his best suit of clothes, crossed busy roads in a dream, penetrating the maze of high streets, hardly knowing where they led. But always he thought of Hannah patiently waiting, and never wavered from his resolve. Had his quest involved hand-to-hand combat with the fire-snorting dragon of Greywalls, he would have welcomed the challenge.

The publisher's office was in a small court spilling from the main thoroughfare, not easy for a stranger to find but, after many false arrivals and enquiries, Brendin at last tracked it down. Inside it was a mahogany fortress, for Jeffries was not one for flimsy style, and here at a great solid desk in the ante-room – heady drunk from the odour of ancient volumes, sat a clerk, laboriously wading through and correcting a manuscript. He placed an inky thumb on the page and looked up with a rejecting frown at the intruder.

'Well, young man?'

'Is Mr Jeffries in?' Brendin enquired, politely.

Jeffries, of course, was always in. His life was his

books – either here or in Crigga, and his death would probably be among them too.

'What might that be to you?' asked the clerk.

'I would like to see him.'

'*You* would like to see *him*?' The clerk wagged his forefinger, sacrificing his previous mark on the manuscript. 'Now, I daresay you would. Eh? Eh?' His voice was a clear replica culled from his master. 'Mr Jeffries sees no-one without an appointment.'

'I *must* see him.'

There was an urgency in Brendin's voice. He had not endured a fate-laden journey for this, and his plea softened the clerk. 'Well, I don't know,' he murmured. 'What's the name?'

'It's Brendin Pendenna – and I've come all the way from Cornwall to see him.'

'Have you, indeed? Well, well,' muttered the clerk, who had never in his life strayed further than Pimlico. 'Well, well,' he repeated, 'I aint making any promises.'

Reluctantly, he abandoned the manuscript and made for an inner door. From within came a verbal eruption.

'What? What? What's that to me? No appointment, eh? Tell him to …' He looked up and saw Brendin standing in the doorway. 'Good God!' he exclaimed. Twenty years earlier, identical features had been framed in that doorway.

'Just a few minutes of your time sir,' Brendin asked.

Jeffries, bluff, florid, sitting at his monumental desk, hesitated, then waved the clerk imperiously from the room. 'Say what you have to say,' he told Brendin shortly, 'then go.'

Brendin advanced to the desk, surprised – now the ordeal was on him – at his own calm. 'You know who I am, sir?'

'Damn me,' growled Jeffries, 'I'd hoped to forget.

You're the fisherman's lad, Pendenna.'

'Or Wickenham,' Brendin looked him straight in the eye, 'Did you also hope to forget that?'

'Christ almighty!' Jeffries slammed a great hand on the desk. 'So, it's some sort of blackmail, is it? Eh? I thought it might come to that. What is it you want, sir? Eh? Eh? By God, you won't get a penny from me.'

It was a typical Jeffries reaction, and an unhappy beginning, but though his heart leapt, Brendin strove to keep calm. 'I don't want your money,' he said tensely, 'any more than I took it when you threw it at me on the path.'

'Ah, *that.*' Jeffries dismissed it with a couple of words. 'Let me tell you, I washed my hands of Wickenham years ago. Don't want reminding of him – doing what he did and then absconding like that to find fame elsewhere. He was a fool, sir – to himself and everyone else.'

Brendin was blind to Jeffries' rage, overlooking the detail in a bid to keep within himself. He breathed deeply and slowly. He had hoped Jeffries might have mellowed through the years, but the cause already seemed lost. He held up his head and looked the publisher straight in the eye. 'I want to marry Hannah, your niece.'

'You *what*?' The face opposite him changed from florid to puce, to a stony grey, then to a sickly white. 'Are you mad, boy? Have you gone out of your mind?' He rose in his ire, shaking a threatening finger. 'A damned fisher-boy, no prospects, no money, no breeding – and you want to marry Hannah? Eh? Eh? Out of my sight, sir!'

'It might please you to know, sir, that I now have an education,' Brendin countered, 'and with that I shall…'

Jeffries tone changed to query, at once aware of the boy's fine suit of clothes. 'How so?'

'I had a fine tutor.'

Jeffries threw his head back and sneered. He fumbled for a cigar, lit it, and sent a cloud of smoke curling upwards.

Brendin stood his ground. 'Please listen, sir, just for a moment. I wanted to do the right thing and talk to you first. Hannah feels the same. We *will* marry, sir, with or without your approval. We love each other.'

'Love? Poppycock.' Jeffries' anger imploded into a deadly calm. He stared at Brendin with an intensity far more ominous than his previous wrath. 'If you want to do the right thing, as you put it, forget this nonsense – for the girl's sake as well as yours. If you killed me first, you would never marry Hannah. Now go, boy. Get back to your fishing. Get out of my office, and God save me – never let me see you again.' And as soon as Brendin was out of earshot he called bluffly to the clerk, 'Get me Mrs James on the telephone. Let's try the worth of this device.'

The conversation was devious and cruel: 'Tell, the wretch, anything you like … No, tell him…' And despite Mrs James' weak protestations, the plot was hatched.

Brendin was disappointed but not surprised at the outcome. The Jeffries of this imperfect world rarely change their spots, though he had offered many prayers that the old irascible would be prepared to talk reasonably, and was shaken by the deep, bitter reaction that had transformed the publisher when he left. The verdict appeared final and irreversible, but he had tried honestly, and surely, despite Jeffries' unquestioned influence, Hannah's mother must have the ultimate say.

With time an important factor, he made his way at once to the arid refinement of outer Belgravia, where the house in Cambridge Street bore a façade of withdrawn Victorian gentility, as if in discreet mourning for an age now past. It would have been a social gaffe to have called without announcement, but Hannah had made some amends by sending a brief note of advice to her mother. But the niceties were secondary now.

A smart little parlour maid answered the ring, and a minute or two later Brendin was shown into the drawing room to meet Mrs James. She was a slim, immaculate lady with a veneer of conventional charm, though beneath it she seemed ill at ease and was clearly highly strung – forever turning, adjusting her sleeves, and nervously fiddling with the rings and necklace she wore.

'Mr Pendenna? Will you be seated? Will you take tea?'

Her speech was precise, tuneful. In this respect alone did she remind him of his vivacious, delightful Hannah. During the polite exchanges, he glanced round the spacious room with interest. This, then, was Hannah's home. He could imagine her daintily moving through it, sitting, perhaps, where he now sat – gazing as he was from the tall wide windows and listening to the muffin man, ringing his bell as he passed by. Then Mrs James was speaking.

'Well, Mr Pendenna, what is the purpose of your visit?' She became more nervous. 'I assume it has something to do with Hannah?'

'Yes, Mrs James, it has.' He paused, half afraid of a further rejection. 'I come from Crigga. Hannah and I have met while she has been staying at the grey – at Greywalls.'

'Yes, I'm afraid that I'm aware of that.'

'Mrs James – I'm not a speechmaker, but I mean this sincerely.' He watched her face harden and she gripped ceaselessly at her rings. 'Hannah and I are in love with each other.'

'My dear boy, she is just a child and – if you will

forgive me – so are you. You cannot possibly know your own minds.' The tone was patronising.

'But we *do*,' he insisted, 'Please understand. We are in love, and I ask your permission to marry her.'

She swallowed hard. 'Marry Hannah? Now, Mr Pendenna, you must surely know that such a thing is quite impossible. Not only your ages, but your background – your lack of prospects. We want far more for Hannah. It is quite out of the question.'

'But why?'

'I have just explained. You are not old enough to know your own minds – and forgive me for saying so, young man – there is an important difference in class. Such a match would be disastrous.'

'I have had a good education – enough to be a private tutor, at least. And I love her. I would work for her, make her happy …'

He pleaded with all the sincerity in his being, but though she listened politely, her eyes widened in genteel horror.

'*Mr. Pendenna.* Enough of this, please. You cannot. It is an absolute impossibility. Please go. There is nothing more to be said, and all this talk is upsetting me.'

He rose unhappily. 'Mrs James, I had hoped that at least you would understand. But whatever you or Mr Jeffries say, nothing will stop us.'

He had reached the door when she called him back, trying to conceal her panic. 'One moment.' Her hands were shaking and there were large tears in her eyes. Her voice trembled and florid blotches crept up her neck.

Brendin stepped forward. 'Mrs. James?'

'Tablets,' she whispered, 'over there – on the table.'

He found them and handed them to her. Shakily, she opened the bottle and swallowed three. Her face was transformed now into shuddering wrinkles, and tears rolled down her cheeks. Then, very slowly, she began to recover some poise.

'I'm sorry,' she said, 'So sorry. Hannah may have told you. I'm sometimes – ill.'

'Yes. Forgive me for distressing you,' he said.

'Sit down again, boy. Please. I can see you love her, and oh, I just cannot bear to see anyone so upset.' She shook her head, clasping her hands again. 'I should like to help you, to make you both happy, but things are not always as they seem …'

He listened intently.

She took another sip of tea. 'Oh, I *am* silly, I should have taken my tablets before. But … Brendin, I should have told you. Of course, I know part of your story.'

'Through Mr Jeffries?'

'Yes. Philip Wickenham was my brother-in-law. We were shocked about what happened. Hannah knows little about him.'

'I've only recently known about him myself,' Brendin began …

'His name is rarely mentioned in the house,' she continued, 'Poor boy, poor, poor boy. You resemble him, of course. I saw it the moment you walked through the door.' She became agitated again, mindful of Jeffries, her words running away with her. 'There is something you have a right – in all decency – to know …'

'Yes?' He was puzzled.

The lie stumbled from her mouth: 'Hannah is not my daughter. I merely adopted her when my sister rejected her…'

A chill went through Brendin. 'Then who…?' he asked, a catch in his throat. He could hardly think.

'She is my sister's child. We adopted he soon after her birth.'

He would not admit the clutching fear to his heart, but

his mouth was dry, and he could barely enunciate. 'And your sister is …?'

'Was,' she corrected. Barely audible now, she rested a sympathetic hand on his shoulder. 'My sister was Catherine, Philip Wickenham's wife, and she never got over his betrayal of her. Now don't you see how impossible it is: Hannah is your father's child – your own half-sister!'

Brendin's first impulse was to get up and leave the house, to absorb alone the shock of the unbelievable. But he felt powerless to move, and could only sit dumbly, dimly sensing as through a fog as Mrs James talked on, registering only the lows that penetrated his consciousness. He listened, but hardly heard as she rolled out her explanation.

'Poor Catherine, dear Catherine. She had always wanted a child, but when Hannah arrived, he was so involved with that – that Crigga girl …'

'My mother.'

'The affair destroyed my sister. Oh, she was never very stable – a family weakness – so she turned utterly against him *and* the child. So that was when I adopted Hannah. She never knew, of course.'

'Oh, God!' Brendin sank his head in his hands. But now that Mrs James had found a way out, she became more confident in the lie and the onslaught was merciless. 'Brendin, he – your father – deeply wronged Catherine. And he wronged you, going off like that …'

Yet another blow to absorb, born from the unleashing of her tongue. He had not recovered when she continued in a feast of words. 'Poor Catherine, dear Catherine. May God forgive him for the suffering he has caused. She died in a nursing home. She never really recovered her senses. She would have killed the child – killed her. You must know this. And Hannah must be told.'

He gazed at her, appalled. 'Then dear God, Mrs James, what am I to say? Even now, Hannah is in Crigga, trusting me, waiting for an answer.'

'She will be sent for and told – in my own way.'

Defeated, he lowered his head. When a wreck is total, why risk further buffeting of the wind on rocks.

'You promise never to see her again?' came at a distance.

'I most solemnly promise.' Overcome as in grief, he could only look on her piteously, weakly wish her goodbye and open the door.

As the door closed, he heard the finale. 'May Philip Wickenham be made to pay for his sins!'

How he got to the pavement he never knew, and he had no idea which road he was taking – stunned with the shock of the incredible. For a while, the full implications of the interview would not register, then gradually came through to him with sickening realisation. Now, the sense of belonging and understanding with Hannah seemed plain to him. But in that same moment, of false realisation, he felt the dull ache of loss. There had been conflict before, he had been prepared to face every all odds for the sake of Hannah – for she had always been the promise and reward at the end of them.

And this renunciation was the second small death of Brendin Pendenna.

RENUNCIATION

Automatically, without knowing where or why, Brendin wandered the streets of London – from Belgravia to Chelsea Embankment, over Battersea Bridge, past the Houses of Parliament and to the arches of Waterloo. All concepts of time, food, shelter, the catching of trains, were completely out of his thoughts as he walked trance-like through the unfamiliar places that appeared – not only in his footsteps – but in the wastes of his stricken mind. It was approaching midnight and rain had begun to fall when he turned from the garish length of the Strand into Villiers Street. Seeking shelter, he found himself among a reeking mass of derelict humanity under the old railway arches. Some leaning against the walls, some sitting, others trying to shed their exhaustion by lying on damp cobblestones.

'Spare a copper for a cuppa tea, young gov.'

He looked round at the speaker. Standing by him was the frail relic of a man, grey-bearded, his face drawn with deprivation and fatigue. His clothes were almost solely shrunken trousers, a waistcoat and a ragged, over-size overcoat. He tentatively thrust out a skinny hand which he immediately withdrew, sure of rejection.

Brendin had lived in poverty for much of his life without ever realising that there could be such hopeless destitution as this, unforgivably obscene with the opulence of the great city so near at hand. With a quiver of pity, he groped in his pocket and gave a penny. The old mendicant grasped the penny eagerly and hurried with a weaving motion to the coffee-stall on a nearby corner.

'Me, me,' came a brief quavering chorus from other needy wretches in the half-light, and he gave out more of his pennies. Most of the derelicts were too far gone in restless slumber or gaping dully into the stony distances of the arch.

The sleepers were pathetic in their attempts to contrive travesties of mattresses from old newspapers, cardboard, or panels of boxwood. Some had their feet thrust into cardboard boxes against the cold. There were women and children among them. Many lay miserably upon the cobbles, others were coiled like reptiles, arms, legs, shoulders, and heads hunched into closed circles, attempting to defeat the chill of the stones. All were a passive rebuke to a society which went its way and allowed such conditions to exist.

Brendin stayed with them all night, wishing he could do something more to relieve their distress – himself exhausted, without much money left, feeling utterly outcast and alone. Again, and again through the long early hours he found himself thinking of Soames, the Mission, and the evangelist's words: 'Not a text down their throat like a cup of tea, but a human application of the Lord's teaching – making them *feel*, at least, that they belong ...'

Soon after dawn, he idly drew a folded card from his pocket and was about to throw it away when he noticed a printed cross at the top of it. Listlessly, he opened it – for the want of something better to do and, in the dim light of the archway, recognised it as the pamphlet once handed to him. The print, with a quotation or two, proclaimed the ventures undertaken by Soames' Mission and, at the bottom, linked with an appeal for funds, was an invitation. 'When in London, why not visit us and see for yourself some of the work we do?' The address was a shady street by Vauxhall.

On impulse he got to his feet, massaged his cramped limbs, and asked a waking soul the way to Vauxhall.

'The mission?'

'Yes.'

'Ah, God bless him. More like the Cap'n, and we shouldn't be a-begging for a few crumbs. But it's early yet for the tea.' Then seeing Brendin determined, he said, 'Over the bridge and keep right along by the river.' He took a second look at Brendin's attire. 'But I don't see as how a gentleman like you is in need.' He adjusted the news sheet that covered him and lowered his eyelids in a mockery of sleep.

There was no need to hurry, but Brendin was anxious to get away from the gloom of the arches and, crossing the bridge at Westminster, slowly made his way along the opposite embankment. A brown mist shrouded the London morning, sombrely reflected in the deeper brown of the swirling river. A tugboat hooted mournfully, coaxing a small crocodile of barges towards the docks. At last, he came to Soames' London Mission. It was a large, square building with no pretensions – a typically non-conformist hall – in an area of ruin as derelict as the unfortunate beings it succoured.

From nearby wasteland human forms began to stir, like the flutter of birds at the throw of a crumb. Soon, one detached himself from the expectant flock and limped across to the mission. After a minute or two he returned more quickly, bearing good tidings.

'They're opening,' he breathed and, as beasts to the trough, they responded to the invitation to eat.

Listlessly, Brendin lined up with the others, and Johnny, a large, friendly man, who had an encouraging phrase for them all, looked at him curiously. He proffered a general ration. 'Buck up me old son, you ain't lost yet.'

Is Captain Soames here?' Brendin asked, after thanking him.

'The Cap'n? Down in a minute.'

In a weary stupor Brendin found a seat at a scrubbed trestle table. The big room was crowded with beggars and dossers in all stages of destitution and disarray, and vaguely he noticed an authoritative figure moving among them at the far end. He drank the tea thankfully then, surrendering to the nausea of sleeplessness and fatigue, cradled his head on his arms. He was just dropping off when he felt a hand on his shoulder and a voice in his ear. The voice changed to concern. 'Why, surely – Brendin Pendenna! You're out on your feet, boy. What are you doing here?'

'It's a long story, sir,' faltered Brendin, rousing himself in relief at having found the evangelist.

'Then we must hear it,' Soames said. 'Come along with me to the office.'

Brendin followed Soames to the end of the feeding area, where a partition screened off an even larger stretch of the hall. In this space were long rows of pallets and blankets in the process of being vacated by groups of pathetically needy. Despite his own troubles, a wave of compassion flooded him. The captain became aware of his glances.

'Yes,' he said, 'we do what we can. The pity of it is that we can't take all of them every night. They must take it in turns. You see I need money, larger premises, helpers. That's why I hurried back from Cornwall. I shall have to give up the circuit, I'm afraid.'

'Who works for you?' Brendin asked.

'Volunteers, mostly. Then there's good old Millie down there with the tea.'

They reached the end of the improvised dormitory, where, opposite other rooms and ablutions, a door opened into an office, a large, lumbered room with a truckle bed in the corner. 'It's young folk we want,' said Soames – young, dedicated folk …' He led the way in and closed the door. 'Now, my dear fellow, sit in that chair and tell me all about yourself.'

At last, Brendin was able to open his heart to a sympathetic listener. He told of his alien upbringing, his puzzlement, his doubts, the discovery of his illegitimacy, of his discovery of his real father …

'God save us! I thought I saw a resemblance, although your father believed you to have died at birth,' interrupted Soames.

'Then he can't be blamed for abandoning me.' Brendin hung his head. 'But all is as nothing to the loss of Hannah and the attendant shame.'

Soames nodded shrewdly. 'Poor boy. I wondered about your story. They should have told you before. Your father …'

'Lives,' Brendin cut in. There was a confused silence, then: 'It was said that he was drowned. All Crigga believed that, but he wasn't. He wasn't drowned in the cove …'

Soames breathed deeply and gave a measured reply. 'Yes, he lived, and it was I who found him, but I had to promise to keep it to myself.'

'Tell me now.

'I found him unconscious on the beach – a distance from the cove …'

Brendin listened as Wickenham's story unfolded – an unending reticule of twists and turns.

'So, he had no choice but to leave – and in a terrible state of anguish,' the evangelist concluded.

'But what about his other child – Hannah? Why abandon her?' Her name was now painful to speak.

'Wickenham confided in me much, but he never told me that Catherine had – was expecting – a child. I don't understand. They were asunder. But she was his wife, and I suppose – well …'

Brendin became pensive. 'They tell me that he was a wicked man,' he said at length, 'but when I read his poetry …'

Soames nodded. 'We are all flawed creatures, are we not? Surely you see in his work a good but tortured soul. Such is a poet. Oh, the bitterness in life, Brendin, my boy. Of *course*, they hate him for what he did. And Jeffries had a professional gripe as well, losing a famous poet for his list – his own protégé – to an American publisher.'

'I can't take all this in, sir.'

'My boy,' murmured Soames, 'you have been under severe emotional and spiritual stress. You must rest.'

'Yes,' and, seeing clearly for the first time, he smiled vaguely as his eyes began to close.

'No more talk, young sir, until you are rested,' insisted Soames.

And Brendin sank down upon the truckle bed and slept.

Soames went about his business and, after several hours, returned with a sandwich and a cup of tea. Brendin roused himself. For a while, had no idea where he was or what had been happening, until the whole sorry business filtered back to him. After a long silence, eating hungrily, he spoke. 'I would like your advice, sir, about something – dare I say – other worldly, something that I find suddenly very confusing.'

'I would say that it's *all* very confusing, my boy, go on – but finish your sandwich first.'

'It's – I suppose you'll think me rather – well – gullible'…

'No, no. What's on your mind?'

'Well, it began when I was quite young. I thought …' He spat it out: 'I thought I saw my father's ghost.'

'Yes, go on …'

The evangelist's credulity was not what he expected,

and Brendin was emboldened to continue. He told of the pull of the cove, the desperate cry of the spectre for Sara, the plea for forgiveness … 'But the question is, 'How could I possibly see the ghost of the living?'

Soames was silent.

'You see the problem?'

Soames nodded.

'I'm sorry, sir – I'm taking too much of your time, and …'

The evangelist raised a prohibitive hand, 'No, no. Let me think about this. There are more things in Heaven *and* Earth, you know – time shifts, telepathy, emotional impressions …'

'I don't understand.'

'Neither do I entirely. But I was in conversation with a learned woman on the subject recently, a woman who was once down on her luck. She told me about her theory – that the soul is more flexible than one would imagine; how, while she was on the street, famished and cold, she had found herself in the vicinity of her old home trying to make amends for a wrong she had done to a brother. She swore to me that she had manifested there, and found him in the garden of her house.'

'Most people would find that difficult to believe. It was a dream,' Brendin suggested.

'My thoughts, entirely – at first. Until she confided that the incident was followed by the brother tracing her and being re-united with her – all as a result of her truly being seen and having a conversation with him in the garden of her home – two hundred and fifty miles from where she really was. Consequently, her problems were resolved.'

'But a living ghost?'

'A seeming paradox, yes, but more like a projection. God truly does work in mysterious ways, my boy.'

'But why would my father appear in the cove – in such distress?'

The evangelist stroked his chin, as though searching for an answer. 'Well, from what I know of Crigga, there's a deal of superstition about the place – paganism and methodism melded together, witchcraft, local legends … It's quite a ferment, wouldn't you say?'

'But I still don't understand why my father would plead with me – when he had no knowledge that I lived.'

'Ah, but perhaps his soul knew. It's all theory, dear boy. It seems that Wickenham had drifted, in thought, to the scene where his life had been in greatest turmoil – physically and emotionally – and somehow his image was imprinted on that scene during the transference of thought. You, a susceptible child had been open to suggestion. I know how distressed your father was, how guilty he felt – *that*, Brendin, *was* indeed, still *is*, his hell.'

Brendin rose. 'Then I must go to him to put his mind to rest.'

'That is not possible, my boy.'

'Oh, but I have some money – I carefully saved from the boat trips – enough for a passage steerage. I want to meet him … What's the matter?'

There was a long pause before Soames tongued words of regret. 'Your father died – only a few months ago, my boy. I read of his sad death in *The Times.*'

Brendin sank into his arms and wept – for Hannah, for his distressed father's wraith, for all the twists and turns of his sad life.

Soames put a hand on his shoulder. 'This grief will pass as all things do in time. You must look forward, boy.' A warm smile broke onto the evangelist's face. 'Do you know what I thought, all those years ago, when you wandered my way as a child and I gave you cake?'

'Probably what a scruffy little urchin I was.'

The evangelist shook his head: 'Be not afraid to entertain strangers, for thereby some have entertained angels, unawares.'

SEPARATION

Brendin sent a message to Daddy Joe by means of his friend, the tutor – telling him that he would not be home for a while. Meanwhile he toiled at the mission, but his thoughts were never far from Crigga. He compared foggy nights by the Thames with the fresh sea mist that curled gently on the horizon; the roaring traffic of the city with the cry of gulls on the swelling ocean; the garish streetlamps with the stars that hung brightly over the bay...

As his thoughts found a way back there, and ventured by the hollow on the headland, he recoiled, erased the image from his mind, for the headland and the hollow meant Hannah – and Hannah was taboo. He must put a further distance from the woman he dared no longer desire. He grimaced wondering – with searing ache in his heart – what on earth she would think and do, for he supposed she knew the truth by now.

Hannah had gone down to Crigga station and waited for the early train from London. Full of excitement as it came rumbling to a stop, she had watched as, one after the other, doors opened, and passengers stepped onto the platform. She stood there for some while, until the steam curled away, and the platform grew silent and deserted. Her heart sank. Where was he? He had promised faithfully he would be there, and she had promised to meet him. He must have missed the early train, she persuaded herself. Disappointment had not yet turned to anguish, and she smiled, for she would feign disapproval when he returned, not speak to him for a full five minutes. But, although she waited, he returned neither on the next train – nor the next...

Greywalls – along with the vicar and local doctor – was one of the first houses to have a telephone installed in Crigga. Later that day, it rang imperiously. Clements answered it at once and relayed the news that Hannah must return in haste to London. The call was abrupt, Clements too eager to help her gather a few essential things together, and Hannah sensed bad news.

As the train pulled away from Crigga, her mind crowded with questions and answers. Had they rejected Brendin because of some petty family feud? If so, she would stand defiant. They would run away together as planned. It was planned and she was wilful … But as the train lurched nearer to London, she became uneasy, doubtful, and down at heart. She was not without cause.

Hannah arrived in outer Belgravia from Paddington by cab, travel weary. Discarding her hat and small case in the hall, she entered the drawing room to find her mother and Jeffries sitting either side of the fire – clearly disturbed in conference. Jeffries rose – a lumbering figure in a cloud of cigar smoke. Mrs James remained sitting – gripping her wrist as though attempting to hold herself together.

'Mother, Uncle Jeffs?' Her tone was anxious.

'Sit down, Hannah, dear. You're tired from your journey, one would think. I'll ring for tea.' Her mother always sent for tea when there was something unpleasant in the air.

'And we'll have a plate of sandwiches, eh?' Jeffries added, ringing for the maid.

'Well, what is this about? Why have I been sent from Crigga?' Hannah demanded.

Mrs James shrank in her chair.

'I think you know why,' Jeffries began …

'You have seen Brendin?' Hannah cut in. 'Has he spoken of our future?'

'My dear girl,' Jeffries stressed, 'you have no future with the boy. You see ...'

Hannah bristled. She had never been afraid of Uncle Jeffries and would not be afraid of him now. 'What I see is this: Brendin and I intend to marry – with or without your gracious permission.'

Mrs James shrank further into her chair, and Jeffries spun the lie. 'Even though he is your half- brother?'

Hannah gasped, 'You can't mean it. I don't believe you. I don't believe any of it.'

Mrs James' strained face emerged into the lamplight. 'You *must* believe it, my dear. You are my sister's child and Philip Wickenham's. As such – the half-sister of Brendin Pendenna.'

In one symbolic huff, the lamp flickered and went out.

As the days went by in mechanical routine, Hannah withdrew into herself. With a feeling of disgust and incredulity, came a sense of grief for the loss of Brendin Pendenna, and the knowledge that they could no longer conquer the dragon. Refusing to eat, unable to sleep and speaking to no-one, Hannah grew pale as she wandered about the house, giving great cause for concern.

'Won't you take some lunch with me, dear?'

'I'm not hungry.'

Mrs James had begun to regret her part in her daughter's unhappiness, and wondered whether she should rein in her lie. But she had been too long under the bullying influence of Jeffries to dare, and now that the Pendenna problem had been resolved she must let it lie. 'I do wish you would get some fresh air, dear ...' she persisted, but Hannah had already gone from the house.

Hannah wandered through Pimlico and down towards the Embankment, sat on a seat by Cheyne Walk, watched the barges chugging and the sailing vessels tacking down river … How easy it would be to slip in, unnoticed, down into the murky Thames. She did not know that Brendin was the other side of that river at Soames' Mission, but she thought of him in her pain, still a small distance from where he was.

Hannah continued to Victoria, where she entered the library by the station to rest. As she sat alone in the corner, someone tapped her shoulder with the handle of a parasol. It was young Myra Pomfret, the pretentious daughter of a family friend. Hannah's heart sank for, in her excitement and unwisely, she had told Myra about her attachment to Brendin on Myra's recent visit to Crigga.

'Hannah James! How lovely to see you! I just came to return my Kipling – with my chaperone over there, of course. Where is yours?'

'I do not have one now. I am almost of age.'

'How exciting. But what a dreadful scandal for you, dear!'

'Scandal?'

'Well, there's always some scandal, isn't there? Without which our lives would be dreadfully dull. But it cannot be true.'

'I cannot think what you mean.'

'Myra cast a knowing look. 'The servants do talk – your maid and our cook … Oh, but I am sure it was only gossip.'

'They have no right to gossip.'

She continued with a cascade of bile. 'But you look suddenly quite pale. Of course, the servants should not gossip – if indeed it is true.'

'But if you are referring to Brendin Pendenna being my half-brother – then it is certainly true.' She was not sure why she let the words fall away from her, the choice information spreading like a virus onto the wings of malice.

'Oh!' Myra sank into the next chair as Hannah rose to go.

'Spare me your mock sympathy. I shall say goodbye, knowing that we shall not meet as friends again.'

Myra leaned on her parasol in disbelief – a parasol that, but for decorum, Hannah would have snatched from her hand and hit her on the head with. Then somehow, she found her way, unseeing, into the street – suppressing laughter and tears in turn.

TRUTH

For the Crigga lovers, the web of circumstance and gossip continued to weave its thread. Only work eased the unspeakable pain of the coming years. To begin with, Brendin volunteered at the mission – afterwards, enlisting as a soldier in the First World War. He returned to the work, after he sustained a minor injury in a gas attack at Ypres.

Paralleled, trying to forget, Hannah worked as an auxiliary nurse, sometimes a breath away from the man she had loved. She would turn a corner just as he turned the next, swing through a door as he swung out, or hurry down steps as he hurried up – in an abortive act of fate.

When the conflict was over, she returned to Belgravia – despite all – and helped to nurse Mrs James, whose veiled guilt led her into – first mental decline, then physical pain.

'I have done great wrong,' murmured the old woman in her death throes, 'God will forgive me, won't he?'

'We have all done wrong in our lives. Rest quietly …'

And Mrs James *came* to rest.

There followed a devastating revelation. After the funeral, when the will was read, the Executor had handed a letter to Hannah. It was written in a frail hand and barely decipherable. Hannah read it when she was alone.

My dear Hannah,

You have been good to me in my illness, and for that I am truly grateful, but I am afraid I have done you a great wrong. I must own that it occurred when I was too weak to withstand the influence of Uncle Jeffries. Now, as I go to my Maker, I must confess that I lied to you, my dear, for you truly are my daughter. You are truly

Hannah James and not Hannah Wickenham as we told you ...

God forgive me, and I hope that you can find it in your heart to forgive me too.

Your loving mother.

'Oh, God!' The room spun, and all the suppressed memories of Brendin – her childhood sweetheart, her love, came flooding back into her consciousness. The loss – and all for the vendetta of others. Pacing up and down the room, she read again, heart pounding, incredulous ...

Greywalls belonged to her now. She would go back to Crigga. Surely, he would be there or one day he would come?

The train steamed into Crigga station. The jingle was waiting in the yard, but Hannah sent it ahead to Greywalls with her luggage. She had no time to waste on tea and pleasantries with aged Clements. 'Tell her I need to take the air,' she told Shaddy, 'And I shall see her soon.'

She hurried, tripping towards the headland overlooking the harbour. Brendin would be hard at work now – maintaining the boat or skippering a trip around the bay. Below her, by the cove, a colony of gulls rose suddenly into an arc, cried out and squabbled when a small fishing craft came sailing in. Her heart leapt as she watched a group of out-of-season visitors being guided from boat to shore. Screening her eyes against the light, hoping for a glimpse of Brendin, for he was sure to be there, she waited. But when at last the group dispersed, Brendin was not among them. An unfamiliar figure made fast the vessel and went away, just as a small yacht sailed into view and tacked out of sight around the bay. She sat for a moment until the last floating seagull had flown back to the crags, leaving the ocean calm and quiet but for the rippling orchestra of breaking waves.

Disappointed, Hannah went down to the harbour and waited, hoping that he might appear. She was looking out to sea when she sensed someone behind her on shingle. She swung round to see Shaddy Bunt standing there with an inane grin on his now crag-riddled face.

'He ent here, you.'

'Who isn't here?'

'He ent,' he said secretively, 'He'm gone a long while. Ent nobody seen 'un.'

'I don't know who you're talking about. I simply came to take the air,' Hannah said. 'And if you don't mind …'

'Clements be waitin'.'

'Then go and tell her I'm on my way.'

'He ent come for years, you,' Shaddy insisted as he turned to go.

Hannah watched him out of sight and climbed the rough-hewn steps towards the Pemberthy cottage, perched like a boulder on the edge of the cliff. She knocked on the tiny door and Phoebe opened it in a sweat.

'Who be 'ee, then?'

'I hoped to see Brendin.'

'Do 'ee be that Hannah James from the grey house, then?'

'Yes, I am. And you must be Phoebe. How do you do?'

Hannah extended her hand but, Phoebe, busy wiping fish-stains on her apron, declined. 'Oh, no, Miss, not till I've washed 'em proper – they'm stinking o' fish. But what are 'ee doin' down-along?'

'Things we need to settle. Do you know where Brendin is now? Do you have his address?'

'No. We ent seen 'un since he left the army.'

'Army? – Oh, well thank you.'

As she left the cottage, Phoebe bobbed a curtsey as though caught in the presence of royalty.

Hannah set out for the headland. She looked out to sea where angry waves came thundering in, crashing against the Reaper Rock, sucking at its great tooth, before curling back ready to strike mercilessly once more. In the spray lifting to the air, she fancied she saw faces – imprints of mariners long lost, and she shuddered. There was something terrifying in this seething sea that hypnotised her. Then she sensed a kraken lurking in the deep – ready to wind tentacles around her fears. But such things had mirrored her poor state of mind.

Every day afterwards, Hannah walked to the headland, to the hollow, to the harbour... in the decreasing hope of Brendin's return to Crigga. Until...

Some years later, when she was in the library of Greywalls sorting out books, young Sophie – the child of a distant relative she had lately adopted – called her to the window.

'Look, there's a poor man sitting on the bench all in the cold.'

Instinctively, with drumming heart, Hannah threw down the book and hurried to the window. She could tell from his aspect that it was Brendin – older, alone, his head bowed in near sleep. As if pre-ordained and in a trance, she left the house and walked slowly, carefully to where he sat. She touched his shoulder, gently, and he opened his misted eyes. 'Hannah?' he gasped, 'dear, dear Hannah!' Then, with a fearful look he pulled back and uttered, 'You must go. You're my sister'...

She grasped his hand and shook her head, 'No, no, my darling Brendin – I am *not*, I am *not!* It was all a wicked lie to part us.'

'Not – not?' he breathed.

'No – *not*. Oh, you are ill. Come with me. Come to your home at last,' and slowly she helped him stumble up the rough track to Greywalls.

The following week, after they had been reunited, Brendin sank into her arms and Hannah mourned – just as the sun rose in brilliance over the tumbling ocean, and a morning seagull cried.

NANETTE ACKERMAN

Nanette Ackerman was born in Cambridge in 1945. She attended stage school as a young girl, was on the stage at five, and later spent a brief spell as a professional singer. Many years later, after training as a nurse, she studied for a diploma at the Hartley-Hodder School of Speech and Drama in Clifton, Bristol. As a licentiate of London Academy of Music and Dramatic Art, in addition to performing, she has worked as a director and speech and drama teacher, helping many young actors with their careers in theatre and film.

Nanette loves animals, nature, and classical literature - particularly Shakespeare and the Romantic poets. She attempted her first play when she was ten. She was subsequently involved in several plays at theatres in the West Country, including the Little Theatre - Bristol, the Playhouse - Weston-Super-Mare and the Rondo in Bath. Her spectacular children's play, *Perils of the Pond*, which once starred Tom O'Connor, was published by Bohemia in 1991. In addition to this, she has given regular poetry readings on behalf of her father, Charles Ackerman Berry, author of the classic, *Gentleman of the Road*, whose colourful childhood is remembered in her book, *Alias Richard Lee: Pictures of a Chaplin Actor* (Redcliffe Press, Bristol). The book was the subject of a play at Barons Court (Curtain-Up) Theatre, London, in recent years - under the title: *Dick and Daisy* – when she played her own grandmother.

The spiritual, *Poems for my Aunt: Touching another World* was published recently by the Wolfenhowle Press, followed by *The Nurse -Keeper* by Blossom Spring Publishing, and subsequently, *Crigga*, of which *Crigga: The Wraiths of Time* – developed from a draft written by her father – is the prequel.

Nanette enjoys giving dramatic readings and talks from her well-received books, and continues to be kept busy writing.

CHARLES ACKERMAN BERRY: 1908-1996
(Author and Romantic Poet)

When twilight moves not man, dry rain shall fall.
When dry rain falls, springs of all life shall die.

Best known for his highly-acclaimed book, *Gentleman of the Road* (Constable, 1978), Charles won the League of Nation's Essay Prize when he was just fourteen, and his first poetry was published when he was sixteen. His other published works include regular articles for *Punch, Wit and Wisdom, London Opinion* and *Cornish Times* during the 1930s and early 1940s. Much of his work (principally his spiritual Root Philosophy and pantheistic poetry) was written while he lived as a recluse in a self-built cabin in the woods at Bourne, Cambridgeshire throughout the 1930s, until the beginning of the war. His short stories: *Stormy Decision, Woman Below, Deadly Move* and *Bitter Return* were published in the press between 1954 and 1956. *To Be a Vagabond* was serialised by Bristol Evening Post in 1968. In 1977 his poetry was published in the *Countryman* and *Country Life* respectively, followed by the first of the *Phoenix Broad Sheets* - edited by Toni Savage: *Senses* in 1977 and *Formula for Humanity* in 1978. *Gentleman of the Road,* which was an immediate success and attracted a good deal of media interest, was published in 1978, followed by *Threshold and Other Poems* - Redcliffe Press, Bristol in 1979, and *Wisdom from the Wilderness: A Selection of Philosophy and Poetry* - published posthumously by Bohemia in 2000.

Significantly, the famous author and Shakespearean historian A.L. Rowse was an admirer of Charles Ackerman Berry's poetry, acknowledging him as 'a genuine poet'.

www.blossomspringpublishing.com

Printed in Great Britain
by Amazon